JOHN MACKAY was born into a Hebridean family in Glasgow. His roots in Carloway on the Isle of Lewis stretch back beyond written records. *The Road Dance*, his first novel, and draws heavily on the influences of that background. MacKay is the STV News anchor and presenter of the popular current affairs programme *Scotland Tonight*. As a journalist he has covered the dramatic changes in Scotland from the Thatcher era to now.

By the same author:

Heartland, Luath Press, 2004
Last of the Line, Luath Press, 2006
Notes of a Newsman, Luath Press, 2015

The Road Dance

JOHN MACKAY

Luath Press Limited

EDINBURGH

www.luath.co.uk

First published 2002
Reprinted 2008
Reprinted 2010
New edition 2015
Reprinted 2016
Reprinted 2017
Reprinted 2019
Reprinted 2020

The paper used in this book is recyclable.
It is made from low chlorine pulps produced in a low energy,
low emissions manner from renewable forests.

The author's right to be identified as author of this book
under the Copyright, Designs and Patents Act 1988 has been asserted.

Printed and bound by
Bell & Bain Ltd, Glasgow

Typeset in 10.5 point Sabon

With love to
Joyce, Scott and Ross
and
In loving memory of my mother, Cathie.
Gus am bris an làtha.

Acknowledgements

Thanks to my faither Alex for the resource of his memory, the MacRitchie sisters for being who they are, *Comunn Eachdraidh Chàrlabhaigh*, Ken and Marion, Lindsey Macdonald for planting the seed all those years ago, Gavin MacDougall for his belief, all at Luath, Paul McKinney and Shereen Nanjiani and Meg Henderson for her time and advice.

Prologue

THERE WAS NOTHING BETWEEN here and North America but a heaving, ceaseless ocean. Two thousand miles of emptiness. This small, desolate bay had been caressed and battered by the unfettered seas since the beginning of time. Sometimes the waves could even claw at the cliff tops. Boulders lay at their base, the debris of an endless struggle between raw sea and rock. Today, though, there was a truce. Today the water gently lapped the shore. But even on the best of days the wind still tugged the hair and murmured in the ear.

The old woman moved hesitantly across the stones. The smooth, round rocks rolled against each other unsettling her step. She had not been here in more than half a century and yet she lived so close that the sounds of the shore were with her every morning when she woke and every night when she slipped to sleep.

The rocks sloped up in a dune behind her before being lost in the reeds and ferns, which in turn were overwhelmed by the grass and heather of the moorland. From the cliffs above, the stones were a smear of off-white between the dark of the sea and the green of the land. Standing on them on the shore they were every shade of white and grey, with speckles of pink, blue and ochre glinting even in an overcast light. The prehistoric history of the island was ingrained in these rocks.

Rain clouds smirred the horizon, but for now the grey mists above were content to drift on. A froth floated on the tide, a remnant of the most recent storm. The white of the foam was stark against the slate of the sea as it swelled against the cliffs and stroked the shore.

Had it been like this on that awful morning when The Skipper scanned the shoreline? Had he sat where she was now? What was it that had made him look? A movement maybe, a stirring that

9

disturbed the rhythm of the tide? Had it been the dying spasm of her baby before the old man lifted his tiny body from the sea?

I

LIFE ON THIS ISLAND was a constant struggle against the raw power of nature. It lay on the very western edge of Europe and was first to bear the brunt of the uninterrupted Atlantic storms and last to feel the warmth of the continental air streams from the south. It was the outpost of the continent, and it had about it the wildness and harshness of the frontier.

Boils of rock betrayed the thinness of the soil; like eruptions on a pale face, they were evidence that this was not a healthy land. The people survived the poor earth and stood against the driving rain and constant wind. With the yield from their crofts, their beasts and the sea, the people survived, and they thanked God for His goodness and sang His praise. The seeds of faith sown in a foreign land in a different millennium had no deeper, stronger root than here, here where the soil was thin but the soul was fertile.

For six days of the week they toiled in the harshness of the land He bequeathed them, and on the seventh day they thanked Him for it. Eternal peace and salvation brought joy to those who believed, although their faces when in church to hear His word showed little exaltation.

This was the only world Kirsty MacLeod knew, but she dreamed of more. There had always been restlessness within her; it was the very essence of her. She read in her Bible of peoples and of lands so different from anything she knew. Her father would enthral her with his tales from the ports he docked at down the west coast and further over to the east. For a girl who'd never left her own district, there was an excitement about all that was beyond her.

Ten years before, a ship had arrived on the sea loch. It had come to take some émigrés away to the Americas. The sight of the ship thrilled her.

'Did God make that, Father?' she had asked in wonder.

'No, my darling, that was made by men.'

'How could men make something so big, Father?'

'It takes hundreds of men to build big ships like that. And they go all over the world. They bring tea back from India, silk from China, tobacco from America. And they take things from here back to these countries. Sadly they take our people away too.'

'A boat like that has been to America, Father?'

'Many times. A boat like that will have crossed the ocean many's a time. That boat you see there has probably been to places like New York and more.'

'But no one ever comes back from New York, Father. Mam told me so.'

Her father chuckled.

'Your Mam might well be right, m'dear. No person might come back from New York, but the ships,' he said with admiration, 'ships like that can come and go to New York as often as the wind.'

'But why do the people not come back?'

'Oh there are many reasons. Money more than anything. It is a lack of money that makes them go and the same that stops them coming back. And a lot of them don't ever want to come back. It's a grand life some of them have over there, better than they could ever have here. There is nothing for them to come back to.'

'But this is home.'

'It comes to us all. We all leave home sometime, it's just that some travel further than others. Home is where you make it. And in America, from what I hear, it's a better place to have a home.'

'Would you like to have your home in America Father?'

Her father was silent for a moment as he looked to the ship before he stooped and swept her up in his strong arms.

'How could I have my home in America while I have my own big girl right here on the island? You're here, your Mam is here and Neil and Annie. This is my home.'

Years on she remembered the bubbling emotions of that day. Young men struggling to contain their tears as their mothers, faces crushed in sorrow, hugged them for the last time. The bewilderment of children too young to understand what was happening, the only certainty amidst the rabble being the instruction they had to hold tight to their tiny bit of luggage. One boy, maybe three years younger than herself, sat on top of a trunk with both hands wound round the handle of a black kettle. She had felt strangely envious of him, knowing the adventure that lay ahead of him. It had been the source of much guilt for her. How did Annie, her twin, love being at home so much, helping her mother, while Kirsty dreamt of being far away? Perhaps she loved her mother and father less, though she knew she loved them plenty.

Rowing boats had taken the travellers from the pier to the boat, and Kirsty had stayed for much of the afternoon watching the embarkation while her father had helped row the boats out. Some would sit waving repeatedly at those they had just left until they climbed onto the ship. Even then, they quickly returned to the decks to look back at the world they were leaving and would continue to do so until it fell away behind the horizon.

There were others, though, having said their goodbyes, who were now looking ahead to their future. Kirsty was captivated by one young woman who had climbed onto her father's boat with only a trunk and a bag. She was travelling alone and no one had come to say farewell. Kirsty had fantasised about who she might be and why she was alone. The woman had sat quietly in the rowing boat and had not looked back once. She had graciously accepted assistance to get onto the ship and then she was gone from view.

Kirsty was only a young girl, but the images and feelings of that day had never left her. Even now she wanted to be like that mysterious woman. She knew that so many who had been forced to sail away longed to return. The songs of the émigrés yearned for home. They may be prosperous in the New World, but home was the island they knew they would never see again, and how they wept for it. Kirsty could not understand why they cried. They may have had to leave to find work, to make a life for themselves, but that they had surely done. Not for them the back-wrenching labour of cutting the peat, lifting the potatoes, scything the hay and gutting the herring; the constant work, from the setting of the fire and milking the cow in the morning to the covering of the embers late at night. Those gone wrote of factories, huge buildings where hundreds, even thousands worked. And when the day was done they were free. She wanted to join the generations who had gone before, to go to the big cities where the letters said the buildings scraped the sky, and jobs and land were to be had by all. It sounded like the land of dreams, a New World for a new life. And whenever she looked to the west Kirsty so longed for that.

She lived near the end of the village road, a few hundred yards from the shore. Like most others in the settlement, the house was a Black House; a single-level dwelling which seemed almost to cling to the earth from which it had been torn. Solid chunks of stone arranged closely, with a thatched roof. It was so perfectly suited to its environment that it looked almost as natural as the moorland itself. In a place where the wind never rested it found the house of rocks a doughty barrier, with the moist earth between the wall cavities forming a final line of defence. Cattle were sheltered at one end of the house and the family lived in the other, separated by a small entrance lobby. Five of them shared two rooms: Kirsty's parents slept in the living area, Kirsty, her twin sister Annie and brother Neil in the only bedroom. The house smelled of peat smoke and strong tea.

Kirsty was a handsome girl and she knew it. She knew that her shy smiles and cheerful laughs kept the boys looking at her for that second longer. Sometimes, when she passed, a group of them would share a confidence, a laugh and a snigger. There was something of the beast about them at times. They would tease her and banter with her. They would boast of the bull they had calmed, the storm they had endured at sea or the haul of fish they had landed. She would listen and she would laugh, but she would never believe.

Her mother told her how lovely she was, how bright her eyes were; 'You have such beautiful red hair,' she would say, as she brushed it at night. Ordinarily it was tied up close to her head beneath a scarf, but at the dances it would shake free and tumble around her shoulders bringing warmth, light and colour to her face, like the sun setting over the sea. And she would laugh and the boys would whoop as they spun her ever faster. And Kirsty would always be spinning and reeling, be it during the winter ceilidhs in the village hall, or in the road dances during the midsummer when darkness barely cast its cloak. And when the boys danced with her, they would hold her as close as they dared in their rough way, and as they sent her spinning onto her next partner their fingers would slip down her arm relishing the touch of her for as long as they could. And although their fingers may leave her, their eyes never did.

Old Peggy thought Kirsty a little too flighty for her own good. Something about the way she carried herself and the way she giggled. But then Old Peggy thought anyone who didn't clad themselves in joyless colours was frivolous. Old Peggy would tell anyone who listened, and because she was an elderly widow and the village matriarch, people did listen. She would even tell Kirsty herself. 'You watch yourself, girl,' she would say.

Kirsty knew what the old harridan meant – closeness to the boys led to trouble. She'd heard the story of a girl in the village who had had a child. It had happened many years before, but the story was still told and retold. Like the flowers of the machair, it flourished in the right conditions. Like as not that would be a wet and wild night with a gathering at a house. The songs would have been sung and the poems and legends spun. The village gossip would be passed around like a communal quaich, often light-hearted, sometimes with a hint of scandal. Then there might be an oblique reference, a question of detail, and the legend of Mary Horseshoe's daughter would blossom in all its tragedy.

Although most had heard it, few were capable of telling it. Those who could had refined their narrative over many years and recitals; each pause had its place, every look and glance laden with meaning, each sigh drawing out the drama. And as the years passed, the storytellers capable of reliving the events of nearly four decades before had diminished in number. Old Peggy remembered. Old Peggy had been there and Old Peggy would never forget, nor let succeeding generations forget.

Kirsty had never known the girl, although her mother lived in a house below the road as it curled back on itself round a rocky outcrop. The Horseshoe, it was called, and the old lady was known as Mary Horseshoe. Kirsty knew her as a quiet, timid woman who would avoid your gaze even as she spoke to you, for all the speaking that she ever did. She was stooped and frail and the story had it that she had been stooped ever since the night her daughter's screams had heralded the birth of a child, a child that no one expected. The girl herself had barely understood what was happening, they said. Only as the months passed had the awful realisation dawned on her as she saw her stomach swell and felt the flutterings inside, and even then she did not know for sure, but guessed from what she had seen of other women. The long tweed skirts and woollen cardigans and shawls had kept her secret until it could be kept no more. She could not even seek help from her mother and the other older women of the village because they did not know and they could not know. It was only when the waters broke and the blood seeped and the pain pushed the girl to hysteria that anyone knew.

In time-honoured tradition, older women from the village came to help. There were no medical textbooks to follow, but there was the experience of generations of women who had nothing to support them but the sisterhood of other women who knew what needed to be done because they had been through the same themselves so often before.

The community helped bring the child into the world, was a part of it as it passed through its life, and stood over it as it was laid to rest in the burial ground.

It had been so different for this child, a boy with a thatch of black hair and lungs that had forced the sound of his cry along the village road. By the following evening there was no more crying to shatter the night. The bastard child was gone, huddled away to the other side of the island. No one knew where he had gone from there, but Old Peggy said he had been taken to the mainland. Instead of watching a child grow to manhood the village saw a legend mature.

As for the girl who had mothered the child, she too disappeared. There were stories of her moving to a family on another island, of her following the child to the mainland, but those who nursed her that night recalled that she had never returned from the wild frenzy of her childbirth. She had been taken away in a cart, huddled in a shawl with her mother's protective arm around her. She had been trembling like a puppy. Her father had not even been able to wave farewell, his love for his daughter soured by disgust. Her disgrace was his shame. He had failed in his guidance of her.

Mary Horseshoe returned the following day, walking up the road from the bridge, her shawl pulled tight around her head to keep out the wind and the questions. She never again spoke of her daughter in public. And even at night in the privacy of the darkness and her home, her husband never asked. Now the only one who really knew where she had gone was Mary Horseshoe and she never said and she never travelled.

No one knew who the father of the child had been. There were stories of the girl's friendships with this boy or that. The pier on the sea loch was a landing place for fishermen from other parts of the country, sometimes even from different countries. And some of the girls would have gathered to work with the fish and sometimes just to watch these exotic strangers with their strange accents and unusual ways. There were those who said that she misunderstood the rituals and had been drawn too far by one of those men from far away. Even darker allegations were hinted at, never uttered, but insinuated by a look or a mumbled mutter. Wasn't her brother a strange one? Whoever he was, wherever he was, the father of her baby was away from her now, abandoning her to her fate.

At the church the minister softly asked for compassion for the girl and prayed for health for the child and said that in time God would reveal why He had allowed such pain. It was not for man to know such things, but to accept that the Lord worked in mysterious ways. For a few moments he had rested his hands on the pulpit, his head sunk below his shoulders as if he was weighed down by the sorrow of it all.

And then he condemned; this was a lesson to all the young, that looking away from the Lord was to look towards Hell itself. And although everlasting torment was the certain end for those who did not believe, there could be a living Hell for those on earth, when acts not worthy of the Lord could lead to heartbreak and suffering. Face away from the Lord and you face blackness even in sunlight. The shame brought upon a household in the village was the work of evil, and the Devil would stop at nothing to ensnare you. Every impure thought, every moment your mind strayed from His Glory, every temptation was Satan grasping to you, drawing you to him, enslaving you. The Lord worked in wondrous ways, but the Devil was never far behind.

For an hour and more he blistered the congregation before him, his eyes scorching from face to face, his chest heaving like bellows to the flame. The flushed red of his neck and face stark against the white dog collar told everyone that this was a Man of God. His voice rose and fell like the stormy sea. The people before him were at his mercy, tossed from peak to trough by the power of his rage against sin. And in their midst sat Mary Horseshoe, pressed against the pew by the force before her.

When he was done and had entreated that the grace and peace of the Lord be with them all now and forever more, they filed out, still trembling. The memory of it burned through the decades. Mary Horseshoe had walked home that Sabbath as so many before, but despite the people walking with her, she walked alone.

In the years that followed many a girl heard the story of Mary Horseshoe's daughter. And if, like Kirsty, the girl was popular with the boys, the story carried a warning. Kirsty understood the message and it left its mark on her as it did the others. Paul had written to the Ephesians of the mystery of man and wife becoming one flesh. The intimacy between man and woman was for marriage alone and for now, for Kirsty, that must wait. She knew she could have her pick of the men, but she wanted none of them. That would bind her to the island.

Iain Ban told her, she couldn't remember how often, of the croft he was to take over from his ailing father, his plans to build one of the new style of houses which were appearing on the island. White Houses they were called, two storeys high with slate roofs and a kitchen with a stove. Iain had his plans alright: more sheep, more cattle and a new loom for the weaving. Iain wanted to have money in his pocket. He made it clear he wanted to have Kirsty too. And Iain Ban was a real catch, a tall powerful man who had the look of the Vikings from whom he was descended. Iain Ban, they called him, White Iain. He was the prime of his generation in the district and the district thought that whoever Iain chose, Iain would have. Who could not wish to be his wife? He would speak to Kirsty after church, he would walk her home from the village store, all the while telling her of what he was doing to his land and the prospects for his beasts. The time would come soon when he would need someone to be there with him and what a life they would have. He didn't say that it would be Kirsty, but his implication was clear; when the time was right he would come for her and the white flags would be out to celebrate their marriage.

Yet he never saw that not once did he make her heart surge. Kirsty knew there would be no marriage to Iain Ban. He was a good man, but he saw life before him stretching no further than the end of his croft. Kirsty's dreams soared like the moorland eagle beyond that, swooping down beyond the croft and over the ocean.

She despaired of the future others saw for her. She was eighteen and it was a surprise to some that she was not already wed. Marriage, though, meant living with in-laws in an already over-crowded house until another home could be built. It meant having children, many children – some women had given birth to ten and more. Not all would survive and many's the time she had seen a woman grieve over the death of a child. To have something so precious growing within you, to feel it move and come alive and then have it denied to you. It could only be like a part of yourself dying, having it torn from you. How did they go on? How could they begin again? And yet they did.

Infant mortality had become less common in the new century, but always there was the unasked question when a child was born, would it survive its infant years? And women died giving birth. Died in agony trying to give birth to a child that couldn't be released from their body. Kirsty could not help but think that they did not live for themselves, that their life was not their own.

Kirsty wanted so much more, believed that there was more to be made of her life. She devoured letters home from family overseas and she knew that was where she wanted to be.

And now, unexpectedly, there was Murdo. Murdo Book, he

was known as. Books were his passion. This was a man who would often walk the twenty miles and more across the moor to town to get books from the public library. Murdo Book would read and read. His was a mind that craved to learn and though his formal education had ended long before, he wanted to know more. His dream of being a teacher had died with his father's passing, but he could still learn. To what end he didn't know, but there did not need to be a purpose to it. The acquisition of knowledge was a pleasure in itself.

Something set him apart from the other boys of the village. Not his looks, though he was handsome enough, but an air. It wasn't sophistication exactly, more a sense of being a part of them but not one of them, something of a loner. He played the shinty, but he was not so inclined to gather at the bridge to yarn and joke the evening away or sup with them in the bothies. Instead he sought older company, talking with the bodachs of the district – the old men, many of them, even in their eighth or ninth decade, still with keen minds and hoards of deep experience of life and the world. They were the pages of his books brought to life; soldiers, sailors, adventurers, men who had seen the best and worst of mankind and the grandeur of God's earth. And he would learn from them.

Kirsty had known Murdo Book all her life, but it took a chance conversation on a late summer's evening for her to see him in a new light, to learn more of this rather distant man. She had been at the potatoes at an old lazybed her father had found on the moor near the cliff edges. She had lost herself as her eyes gazed at the sea and her mind sailed across it. People from the village, from the island, from the Highlands as a whole, had been crossing that ocean to the Americas for two centuries and more. It had been for adventure at first, young men following the sunset to find adventure and riches. Too soon, though, it had become necessity as clan chiefs, once paternal kin, had been seduced by the good living of the south. Blood, kinship and loyalty paled against a lifestyle of fine wine, good food and status in genteel society. In Edinburgh and London the ancient bonds of ancestry and loyalty were as nothing compared to the cosmopolitan sophistication of the lords and ladies. The chiefs had turned away from their people, without whom they would be nothing. And after turning away from them, they turned upon them. High living came at a price and land could provide a better return than people, particularly if that land was filled with sheep. Sheep could be sold, humans could not. The clan chiefs became landowners whose right to possess the land was lost somewhere in the mists of genealogy. The people were burned from their homes and cleared from the land. Thousands were forced across the ocean out of sight and out of conscience. Kirsty knew of these people, and of the bitterness that endured three and four generations on.

Even now the clearances continued, but in a different way; now it was an economic imperative. With limits on the good land available, younger sons saw emigration as their only chance of prosperity. Men who might have anticipated a life of working with the plough and the scythe and the fishing smack, crossed the Atlantic and became familiar with the drill and the grinder and the production line as they worked in the factories of Detroit and Chicago producing the new motor cars.

Murdo Book had seen the solitary figure looking out to sea. When he came closer to her he said her name.

'Kirsty.'

She was so lost in her fantasy she didn't hear him. He came within a few feet of her.

'Kirsty. Hello.'

She whirled around in surprise.

'Oh Murdo!' she exclaimed.

He moved towards her, his right hand held out in apology.

'I'm sorry if I made you jump.'

Her head bowed and she rubbed her hands distractedly down the sides of her legs, agitated that he had come upon her when she was dreaming her dreams. She had been so absorbed that she did not know how long she had been there. How long had he been watching her? Had she perhaps spoken aloud in her trance? She felt distressingly vulnerable and exposed.

Throngs of her hair hung heavily over her flushed face. He thought her the most beautiful vision he had ever seen, so alive, so vivid. He had always thought of her so. She brought colour and life to everything around her. But he had understood that she was beyond him and although his heart could still jump when they met, his pulsing arteries remained concealed.

He could not understand the intensity of her reaction. Why was she so overwhelmed? She had only been looking out to sea.

'Were you digging for pirate's treasure?' he smiled, trying to put her at her ease.

'No, I was...' she paused in total confusion. 'The potatoes.'

Murdo looked to the horizon.

'It's a lovely night, is it not?'

'It is. It's beautiful,' she said, regaining her composure.

'There's not a cloud in the sky. You could believe there's not a cloud between here and America.'

Below them the sun blazed a golden road westward across the sea, shimmering to bronze and copper before the light was lost to the shadows of the brooding rocks. The sea was settling in before nightfall glided over it with darkness and unknown fears.

'It can take weeks to sail that ocean,' Murdo said quietly, 'and when you reach America there is much the same distance of land until the Pacific. They've got too much land and not enough people to fill it.'

Kirsty lifted her eyes to the horizon. The two of them stood with their backs to the old world, the world they both knew so well. Behind them were the blackhouses and the crofts, the peat stacks and the church at the end of the road. As they stood together the sea breeze that brushed past them seemed to carry with it new life from beyond the horizon. They both shared the same dream and they sensed that they were with a kindred spirit. The final glow of the ebbing sun seemed to forge a bond between them as it gently lowered the island into dusk and proffered dawn to the land of promise.

'I'm going to go there,' Murdo said. 'There is nothing for me here. Whatever I do I will always be Murdo, son of Calum, son of Murdo. I have the same name as my grandfather and I live in the same village as my grandfather and his father before him. In their lives the world barely changed. They had as much here as they would have had anywhere else. But the world is changing, it's exploding, and it will never be the same again. This is all happening now, but it is happening somewhere else.'

Murdo spoke of his plans to go to America, but not as others had, simply aspiring to work for someone else. In America Murdo was going to be his own man, in control of his own destiny in a way that would never be possible at home.

He became more intense, staring from the sea to her eyes. And she was drawn into his excitement, swept along in his vision.

'On this island I will always be who I am and I will always do what I do. If I move to the mainland or down to the cities I will always be a man from the islands and they will judge me by that. But in America it doesn't matter who I am or where I'm from, it's what I can do that counts. And if I can do it for myself then all the better.'

Kirsty was entranced. It was as if he had been reading her mind. She had known Murdo all her life, but as a distant, peripheral figure. But his words made her heart pound with exhilaration. His mind so quick, so keen and his eyes so dark and intense. For all the dreams Kirsty had of a new life, there had always been the doubt that for a woman it may not come to pass. She'd considered two possibilities of passage. Some women had travelled over to become the wives of men they had never met, men who had emigrated before their future wife had even been born and who now sought a partner. A partnership was what it would be: such a man would have spent his early years building up a farm, and his woman would be there to provide a home and a family to take it on. The other possibility was to answer one of the occasional advertisements in the post office offering emigration for women who would work as maids to wealthy families. Neither choice appealed to Kirsty's independent spirit. She reasoned that if she was to work in service she would be as well working for a husband with whom she might have no affinity but who could at least provide security. But if that was the best choice, then it was no choice at all.

Now Murdo Book seemed to be offering a different way, though perhaps he didn't even realise it himself, but she sensed it in the way he was opening up to her.

She wanted to tell him of her own dreams, but he was gushing like a burn in spate and there was no stopping him. He had an uncle in New York who was something of a hero to him. He was the brother of Murdo's mother and he had sailed away before the century had ended, before Murdo had been born. Uncle Alasdair had gone first to Toronto in Canada and then to the motor factories in Detroit. Now he was in New York City working as a joiner. He was married, but had no children and regarded his sister's family as his own.

He only knew him through his letters home, but Murdo had always been able to sense him, feel his presence, hear his voice. From before he could read, Murdo remembered when the regular letter from his uncle arrived. Even the knowledge that the thin, pale blue envelope with its large stamps and address written in bold, sweeping strokes had come from so far away was a thrill in itself. His mother would not open it until the family was gathered together. Then, with no little ceremony, she would carefully slit it open and start to read, slowly and hesitantly, sometimes having difficulty making out a word. It would be written mostly in Gaelic, but his language of common use was English, so he would skip between the two.

Murdo, more than any of his siblings, was hungry for the news from overseas. If his mother paused while she tried to make out a word, the interruption in the flow was almost too much for him to bear. And if his mother would read under her breath something she wanted withheld from the children, his irritation was absolute. As he learned to read for himself, Murdo would be allowed to read the letter. This he would do, over and over again. Uncle Alasdair would ask about the people and the life at home. He still felt a part of it even though he was so far away. He would write of his regret when he heard of someone passing away. He would know when the cows were to be taken out to the moorland pastures over the summer. But Murdo would become really immersed when Uncle Alasdair wrote of what he was doing himself. He spoke of dollars, of streets and avenues that had numbers not names, of automobiles and apartments. Murdo knew that in Glasgow there were houses that were four storeys high. Uncle Alasdair wrote of buildings that had fifty levels and more. And when at the end of his letters Uncle Alasdair asked after the children, Murdo would be thrilled to see his own name written there by this man who had seen and done so much.

Murdo told Kirsty that he would live in New York City. Uncle Alasdair had written telling him to come and stay, telling him that he too could be a part of the American Dream.

'Too many folk who come here can't even speak English,' Uncle Alasdair had written. 'You can't fail. They want bright lads like you. You can stay with me until you find what you want to do. I could even fix something up for you.' Murdo so wanted to go, but he was the eldest in a family without a father and he felt the burden of responsibility. His mother understood his dilemma. Her own brother had gone before and made a good life for himself. Murdo's father may be dead, but she had told him that she would not stand in his way.

The sun had long disappeared below the horizon by the time Murdo's cascade subsided. In its place were myriad stars, millions of them and more. Every detail of the night sky was clear to the naked eye. A rock just a footstep ahead was lost in the gloom and yet the gleam from a star light years away was as bright as rock crystal. In the darkness Kirsty too began to voice her dreams.

'I have fancied that someday I too would go there. I hear of women who work over there, not on crofts or in houses, but in banks, in shops and in businesses. I could never do that here. But in America I surely could.'

Murdo was enthralled by her quiet determination. No woman had ever before confided in him like this, and it thrilled him.

'You say you have your grandfather's name,' she continued, 'but one day it'll be your own name. And your children and their children will be known by your name. Me? I will never be me. I was born my father's daughter and even now that is what I am. Should I ever wed I will become the wife of Peter, Kenny, Iain or whoever and even when they die before me that is all I will ever be: a daughter, a wife, a mother and a widow. Even when I die I will be buried with my father's name above me. I will never be me. That is my past, my present and my future. But I want more and maybe I will only ever find it if I leave behind all that I know and all that knows me.'

The first chill of the night made her shiver. Murdo slipped off his jacket and draped it over her shoulders. This was the first physical contact there had been between them. But they had talked with a vitality as intense as any first kiss.

They began to make their way off the moor down to the shore, carefully navigating their way across the rocks. Kirsty giggled gently when Murdo stumbled. Further on he turned to help her climb down from a steep rock and though she had done so often herself, she did not reject his attentions.

They came onto the village road. Although they could barely see ahead of them, they did not stumble. This was a road both had known since birth.

'How would you go?' he asked her. 'Where would you go?'

'It is a dream for now,' she sighed. 'The real world just spoils the dream. But maybe my chance will come some day.'

Too soon they reached Kirsty's house. She shrugged off his jacket and held it out to him. He tugged it on and hesitated, biting his lip.

'Kirsty. You could come with me if you wanted,' he said haltingly. 'We could go together.'

Her heart leapt. She had wanted him to say just that.

'Oh Murdo! But how can I?'

Murdo gently grasped her arm and she felt the softness of his lips on her cheek and the warmth of his breath on her face. She turned to face him and saw the whites of his eyes stark in the gloom. The glint on his iris could have been a flash from the stars. He brought both hands up to her face and cupped her head in them. Gently and deliberately he kissed her lips. She couldn't close her eyes and nor did he. His gaze held her as he caressed her.

He whispered, 'We'll do this together.'

And then he was gone, his boots scrunching on the stones of the road. And yet it felt to Kirsty as if his hands were still on her. The damp of her lips caught the cool of the wind. She became aware of the sound of her heart thudding and that her fists were clenched and her arms bent almost as if to protect her. With a sudden sigh she relaxed, glanced about her, and hurried down the path to the house.

What had happened? She had been digging the earth with a cromman to gather potatoes in a bucket. There was the prospect of tea and a blether with the family about the day's events. Tomorrow she would have expected another day much the same. Yet now she felt herself alive as she had never been before. She knew she was in love, her senses tingling with the anticipation of something unknown. She saw her future clear before her, dazzling her and thrilling her.

And how she missed Murdo, though he was scarcely gone from her. This man whom she had always known and yet never really known until now. He had been a figure in the village, a boy she'd known all her life, a man she'd danced with, and that was all she had ever thought of him as being. Now she was helplessly in love with him because he had shown her what could be. And he had kissed her, not some childlike kiss with tightly closed mouth against a half-turned cheek, but a real kiss that lingered on her lips and left her weak. She longed to chase after him, to be with him, to walk into the night with him. Kirsty felt as if she'd been reborn.

As he walked further away, Murdo could barely believe what he had done. He had strode away quickly, stunned by his own impulse, fearing her reaction. His neck was tense with apprehension. Hadn't this girl just been telling him how she wanted to make a life of her own, free from constrictions and expectations? And what had he done? He had grabbed her, kissed her and told her they could do it together. But desire for her had swept over him. This girl stirred something in every male and he had been no different. He'd watched the way men looked at her at the dances, even at the church, but he was Murdo Book and she would never be interested in him. And yet tonight, she had revealed something of her soul. Her words had seemed to beckon him. It had been too much to resist. However, as he walked on and the fear that he had misjudged everything receded, Murdo began to allow himself to relive his enjoyment of this night. The memories he would always have. Tomorrow was another day.

The creak of the door heralded Kirsty's arrival home. The scene was one that had been part of her life for as long as she could remember: the peat fire glowing, Mam and Annie knitting, father sitting peacefully sucking his pipe in his corner, with his Bible lying on a small shelf by his hand. He was waiting for the whole family to gather together for the Books. Now that Neil had returned from repairing fishing nets and Kirsty had come back from the lazy beds, they sat together taking turns to read from His Word and bowing together in muttered prayer. Tonight it meant more to Kirsty than ever it had, because she knew now that it would not be a part of her life for much longer.

Mam asked what had kept her so long, and she heard herself saying she had wanted to watch the sun set. Her mind was wondering where Murdo was now. When Mam had asked had she seen anyone coming in the road, she could only think of what he might be saying as he arrived home himself. And when asked where the pail of potatoes was, Kirsty just didn't hear.

She lay in bed beside her sister that magical night and thought of Murdo, and the future that lay before them. Some in the village had the second sight, a foreboding of what was to come. It was a sweet blessing that Kirsty did not, for she would have seen that before the year was out Murdo would have left the island to fight in the bloody, muddy fields of France and she would have a baby growing within.

2

AS MURDO AND kirsty dreamt of their new life in the west, darker skies were gathering in the east. The killing of the heir to the Austro-Hungarian throne passed unnoticed by most. Political alliances forged between the European powers were just politics played out in capitals far away. But the political coalitions began to pull the nations inexorably towards war as if the hand of doom was scrunching up the map of Western Europe. Even those on the very edges were getting dragged in.

For many young islanders the shillings paid for signing up to the Militia supplemented their incomes from crofting and fishing. Hundreds had joined the army's reserve forces and spent weeks of summer training on the mainland. The islands had a strong tradition of providing fodder for the imperial battlefields. They had a reputation as good warriors and there was no great political cost to their sacrifice. For the young men going through their paces each summer there was little thought of war. They needed money and this was one way of earning it. The great battles belonged to the century that had just died. It was a new world.

Murdo was one of these men. He was the eldest in a family of five. His father had been lost at sea, leaving the family to struggle in tragically common circumstances.

The fishing was a hard life and a dangerous one too; every generation lost some of its men plundering the teeming shoals of herring in the Atlantic. They had fished for generations. They knew the waters and they recognised the changes in the sky. But sometimes the shoals were far out, and the fishing boats had to follow. There had been many a desperate race for the shore as the black clouds formed on the horizon and drove mercilessly towards the land. Boats had been smashed on the cliffs that heralded home, others had been engulfed by the wall of waves, and it happened too that as the boats were tossed and pitched someone would be thrown into the water. Many refused to learn to swim because it would prolong the inevitable. Desperate survival instinct would make them swim but they would know when their strength was sapping and the sea was sucking them down. If you could not swim it would be over sooner. 'Lost at Sea' was the epitaph on many a gravestone with no body beneath. It had been the same for Murdo's father.

Murdo remembered the torment of the night well. The village folk gathered in the whipping wind above the pier on the sea loch, lighting big fires as beacons to guide the fleet home to them. The hope that the intermittent flashing of a lantern in the heaving darkness might be the boat with his father aboard. The disappointment when he was not among the exhausted men stumbling off the boats into the arms of their loved ones. Sitting until the dawn came and the fires failed and the ocean calmed. Comprehending that his father would not be coming home. It was the night he became a man.

The responsibility was on Murdo to help his mother provide for the family. He took on what his father had left behind, the crofting and the shepherding, which provided the barest sustenance. The Militia provided some much-needed cash. There might be a price, but like the others Murdo assured his mother it would never have to be paid. Nevertheless, if the buff envelope arrived calling him to arms, there would be no alternative. Murdo Book would have to take up arms.

Murdo saw Kirsty the morning after their walk on the moor. There had been little doubt he would for it was the Sabbath, and all but the ill and the infirm made their way to the church at least twice in the day. It was the Lord's Day, a day to glory in Him. Food was prepared the night before, shoes polished and everything readied so that nothing would interfere with the worship of the Lord and contemplation of His Word.

Murdo had slept fitfully, his mind restless and dancing. She had turned to him after he had first kissed her. Turned to him, not away. Surely that held a promise? There was little he could understand, save that Kirsty had inflamed in him a surge of something he had never known before. He had read of love and lust, one so wonderful, the other coarse and raw. There had been nothing vulgar in what he had felt, nothing that made him feel ashamed. He had been overwhelmed, but in a way that brought his senses alive and made him tremble so vitally. It had not been a thrill in the way that his first smoke had been, or his first surreptitious drink. It had been instinctive. It had been pure. He felt some embarrassment at his impulsiveness, but no shame in what had roused it.

He had sat with his mother and brothers and sisters. Kirsty was across the church sitting a few pews in front of him with her own family. Her hair was pulled up beneath her beret, but he could see the fringe of red transform into a vivid aureole in the sunlight that poured through the long windows. She would have known he was there, but she never looked for him.

He heard nothing of the minister's sermon. He watched her stand, head bowed for the prayer, followed her fingers flicking through her Bible for the readings. As the congregation praised the Lord through the psalms of David, each voice was lost amid the distinctive wailing of a congregation following the *a cappella* lead of the precentor with myriad minute variations. The sound was at once haunting and beautiful. But he was lost in her, absorbed by the sight of her lips, the glimpse of her teeth as she mouthed the words, her eyes cast down. Not once did they turn to him, not so much as a glance.

At the sermon's end, the congregation shuffled out, heads nodding acknowledgements and voices whispering greetings. The after-service conversations outside the church were as much an arena for gossip and news as the village stores and bothies. Without moving his head, Murdo's eyes followed Kirsty filing down the far aisle. Still she did not so much as glimpse at him. Had he shamed her so greatly last night?

His eyes searched for her instantly he stepped out of the church. It had been but a few moments since he'd lost sight of her, but he felt a tingle when he saw her again, standing in a knot of people with her parents. Now that she was out of the church she was looking for him too, her eyes fixed on the church door watching everyone coming out. When he appeared she smiled at him and then turned her head back to the conversation. She had smiled. She had smiled. He wanted to rush to her, but he knew he would have to bide his time.

A group of the village men were in deep discussion. He had made a habit of joining them, listening to them and learning from them. Today the preliminaries of the theme of the service were quickly disposed of. Other matters were to hand.

'The Kaiser's declared war on the Czar,' said Calum Boer gravely.

He was an older man whose experiences stretched beyond the district boundaries, a legacy of serving in the African wars.

'I came back from town last night and that was the word over there. It's war for sure now.'

He looked at Murdo.

'You can expect your call-up lad,' he said. 'Over there, fighting the Germans. They've been wanting it for a long time.'

' Let the Germans and the Russians sort it out themselves,' said Murdo quietly.

Calum Boer grimaced.

'You can be sure that won't happen. The French will be there and we'll get hauled in too. It's been building for a long time. We might think history is history, but the Germans and the French have always been at each other's throats, and the changing of the numbers of the years doesn't change that.'

'Well let them get on with it,' repeated Murdo.

'If one's in, we're all in, lad.'

'You might even pull on the old kilt again yourself, Calum,' laughed another of the men.

There was a jocular murmur among the group, old men declaring they would be able to take up arms against the Germans and show them what for.

'It'll be good for you, lad,' said another old fellow. 'Good to get away for a while. See another part of the world. You'll not be away for long and you'll have money to send back to your mother.'

Murdo said nothing.

Others had heard the rumours and pressed Calum Boer to tell them more. There was no apparent fear or foreboding. Who would the King call on to fight first? Why, the warriors from the north, who had served so well before. Having heard all that Calum could tell, the young lads bragged of their training in the Militia and how they were ready for anybody. On another day they would have mimicked the marching and squared up to each other in mock aggression, but they kept their joshing in check because of the day it was and where they were.

The Reverend MacIver could sense the buzz and felt some resentment that the message he had delivered to them so powerfully had so quickly been forgotten. This was his domain and he should be the focus of their attention. He approached the throng.

'And what, gentlemen, could possibly be overshadowing the Word of the Lord on this, His day?'

'News of war, Minister,' said Calum Boer.

'War?'

'Indeed. The Germans, the French, the Russians, and ourselves likely as not.'

'I have heard of no such thing.'

'It was the word in town yesterday, Minister.'

'Ah yes, so you came back from town last night eh? I think the Word on which we must concentrate our minds is the Word of God. And if what you say is true, then He will guide us through whatever tribulations are set before us.'

Murdo drifted away. He had heard enough. The news had unsettled him and chilled the glow that had been with him since the night before. He wanted to get away from the talk of war and the banter of his contemporaries, as if putting a distance between the words and himself would make them less real. It was only talk, after all, and he did not want to confront the implications of it now. He wanted to feel good again. He wanted to be with Kirsty.

The congregation was drifting home. Old women walked down the road, arm in arm, always deep in conversation. Their breathing patterns barely affected the stream of chat, as they continued talking even as they inhaled.

Some of the men took the chance to roll a cigarette. They were not all quite as committed to the Sunday rituals as the women folk. There were zealots, certainly, but many of the men, although believers, welcomed the moment of escape from the oppressiveness of the church environs. Once on the road home they enjoyed the chance to talk and gossip. The cluster of black-clad worshippers slowly fragmented, leaving the minister outside the church with his elders. They would be back again in a few hours for more of the same. There was so much sin and he was the man to show them the Way.

Murdo saw Kirsty a little way ahead, walking a few paces behind her mother and father. Her head was bent forward and he saw the paleness of her neck against the drab black coat that hung so shapelessly from her. His heart was thudding hard as he came within two steps of her.

'Aye,' was all he could say.

Kirsty smiled and let him fall in beside her. There was a gentle blush to her cheeks and she kept her head tilted forward and her eyes on the road. When she looked at him, it was the quickest of glances.

'I'm sorry,' he whispered hesitantly. 'I'm sorry for what I did.'

She smiled broadly and her eyes glowed.

They walked a few more steps in silence.

'I maybe got carried away,' Murdo continued, struggling for coherency. 'But I'm glad I did.'

Murdo, although encouraged by the smile, was made uneasy by Kirsty's reticence. Maybe she didn't want to talk about it, maybe she just wanted to forget it. But the smile, the smile hadn't said that. If he walked with her much further he would draw attention, but neither could he walk away from her with nothing, no understanding.

'I'm glad too,' she said at last, with a nervous, muted laugh.

'I would like to see you again.'

'You're seeing me now,' she teased.

'You know what I mean.'

'I know,' she giggled gaily. 'I would as well.'

Her mother looked round. She said nothing, but stared at her

34

daughter before looking ahead again. Their moment had passed.

'By the black rock on the shore,' he murmured quickly. 'Seven o'clock, on Wednesday.'

'Yes.'

'I'll see you.' With that he was gone from her side, his hand ever so quickly brushing hers. Kirsty instinctively gripped her fingers and held her hand against her stomach. Wednesday seemed so far away.

Kirsty's mother turned to her again.

'What was Murdo Book wanting?' she asked.

'He was just saying hello,' Kirsty answered, unconvincingly.

'Was he indeed?'

It was a mild admonition. Kirsty's step became lighter. Her father said nothing. He kept walking. He had an idea why she had been late home from the potatoes the previous night. She might now remember where she'd left the bucket.

Before the next Sunday their world had changed. On the Tuesday, Great Britain declared war on Germany. By the Wednesday, it was the talk of the village, though Kirsty paid little heed to talk of the Kaiser and the King, cousins both. It didn't concern her. Her thoughts were of Murdo and the evening ahead, her only anxiety that he would be there. She let the clock chime the quarter to the hour and soon after she glided unnoticed away from the house and almost skipped the short distance to the shore, dancing across the stones to the black rock, so splendid and resolute.

Rather than striding down the village road which would take him directly past Kirsty's house, Murdo had gone down his croft and made his way across the moor to the shore. He was in a turmoil of emotions; excited at the prospect of seeing Kirsty, anxious that she might not be there, and uneasy about the news. Britain's declaration of war could indeed force him away if the generals decided the regular army needed reinforcements. And what then?

She saw him coming down off the moor on the south side of the bay where the rocks and earth seemed to slink from the sea rather than roar out of the water with the dramatic defiance of the cliffs opposite. She made her way across the shoreline to meet him, her feet causing the stones to clack as she went. Already she wanted to run to him and to throw her arms around him, still not fully understanding why it was that she now felt such a bond with this man. One conversation, one kiss, and she now she felt as if she would rather be with no other. Running on the stones with any elegance was impossible, and anyway Murdo was cautiously descending the sharply sloping grass before stepping onto the rocks.

When at last they were face to face, he looked behind her to the track up to the village before shyly taking her hand and kissing her cheek. Kirsty slipped her mouth round to his and kissed him full on the lips as if to say 'don't be bashful now, Murdo Book'. As they kissed he watched her red hair cavort in the wind and her smiling eyes close ever so delicately. He brought his free hand to her cheek and as his own eyes closed he breathed the scent of her and thrilled to her softness. And there as the breeze danced around them and the sea purled beneath them they unveiled their love for each other. Doubt and uncertainty between them could be cast away. Whatever lay ahead, this at least would endure.

They sat watching the ocean, her head resting on his shoulder and fronds of her hair playing on his face.

'You know I may have to go?' Murdo said softly. She tensed perceptibly.

'But why?'

'We're at war.'

'I know, I heard my father say. But why would you have to go?'

'I'm in the Militia. If they call you have to go.'

'And will they?'

'I don't know. I thought I should tell you, so that you know. But I'll know soon enough. Let's just enjoy the moment.'

The evening slipped past as they kissed and caressed and talked. He had laid his jacket on the ground and she lay on her back, he beside her, propping his head up on his arm.

'We could travel down to Glasgow, and on to Greenock. Boats sail from there to the Americas and the cost is not so great.'

'Murdo, I so want to go with you, you know that. But how can I? My father would not allow me to just go off on my own.'

'But you wouldn't be on your own.'

'He's even less likely to let me go with you. Not just you, but any man. He just wouldn't have it.'

'You wouldn't go without his permission? What of all that you said about breaking away from what being a woman means here?'

'I know, and I do believe that and want that. But I couldn't just run away. I couldn't do that. It would hurt my mother so much, and my father. I love them too much to do that to them. But I still want to go.'

'Well, how could you? Would they ever give you their blessing?' Murdo was sitting up now and his voice was not so soft.

'I have been thinking about that and I think there would be only one way.'

'And what would that be?'

'I think they would let me go with a husband. If my husband was going they would not try to keep me back.'

He turned toward her again, the grimace gone from his face, leaned over her and kissed her.

'Well then we must get married.'

She threw her arms around his neck and squealed with delight.

By the week's end Murdo's buff envelope had arrived. So soon, he reflected bitterly.

'They have paid me long enough and now I'm theirs,' he said to his mother.

He had to report to the barracks at Inverness. It didn't say, but thereafter he knew he was destined for France. He was not alone. Other young men in the district had received a similar summons. For most, the formal instructions were their passage to adventure, but not for Murdo. He was obliged to be strong for his mother. She had already lost one family leader and couldn't bear the thought of another being denied her.

'They're saying it'll be over by Christmas, Mam,' he reassured her. 'And we could do with the extra money.'

'War is war, my dear,' she said. 'It might be over quickly, but

37

war is war and men are killed.'

She packed an old bag for him. He didn't want his trunk, he had told her, he wouldn't be needing too much. It was a trunk she herself had used as a young woman when she and the other girls followed the fishing fleets to the east coast and to Shetland. They would be away for the summer months and the kist would hold everything for them. It always came back with her and she hoped it might have good fortune for her son and bring him back to her.

'I can't take it with me to France, Mam,' he chided gently.

She knew he was right, but it would have brought her some solace to know that he had it, and that when he looked at it at night far from home it might bring him the comfort that it had brought her. But it was to be a bag and she knew that made sense. There were tears in her eyes as she washed and pressed his clothes.

She feared for him, not just his physical safety, but for his emotional wellbeing. Murdo had always been a sensitive boy. He had never backed away from the rough and tumble as child, but she always knew that his heart was never really in it. When he went off for the summer training with the Militia, it was not with the exuberance of the other lads. He did it because he believed he had to. She regretted that he'd had to grow up so quickly. After his father was lost he had taken on responsibility. But he had always been happier with his books and his thoughts. War could crush such gentle spirits. She prayed for not just for his return, but for the same thoughtful, caring, young man who was leaving to come back. Her son would surely come back a harder man with darkness in his soul.

In houses throughout the district, mothers fussed over the sons who would be leaving. Clothes were washed and bags packed. In almost every one, a Bible or passage of Scripture was tucked away in the belief that it would perhaps protect and certainly comfort their boys. In some homes, the young men talked into the night with their mother or father making the most of the time they had left. Stories from childhood were retold and plans for their return from the battlefields discussed. For some they would be the first in the family to have left the island, and fathers tried to offer wise counsel. In other homes little acknowledgement was made of the impending departures. It meant a baring of emotion that they could not stand.

Prayers were said at special church meetings. The minister and his elders visited the home of every conscript and prayed for his safe deliverance. The people could offer little to their young men other than love and prayers, but they gave generously of both.

Plans were afoot for a Road Dance. Supplies of drink were organised and accordions, fiddles and bagpipes brought out. It was to be the most memorable ever. The young men leaving for war were to be done proud. They would leave with their hearts warm and their spirits high from the cheers ringing in their ears. The Road Dance was to be held the night before the boys left and it would be a ceilidh to remember. Only to be outdone, they said, by the one that would be held when the boys returned safely.

In the midst of it all, Murdo sought out Kirsty.

'You're going, aren't you?' she said, tears blurring the sharpness of her eyes.

'Yes. But not just yet. We have this time together.'

They walked away from the sounds of the village and beyond the cattle on the moorland pastures, until all that could be heard was the sibilance of the sea and the breath of the breeze. There was a rock here that was his place of solitude, worn concave by the winds and the rains into a natural seat. From it he would look onto the sea and imagine beyond the horizon. He had been returning from this place on that first evening, and it was there that he was taking her now.

As they walked hand in hand, she asked him about his call up and when he was to leave. He had told her what he expected, but it was not until they were seated at the rock that he spoke of their future together.

'We will still go,' he said pulling her head to his chest. 'When this is all over we will still go.'

He played his hand through her hair, stroking the long strands and feeling them smooth between his fingers.

'I'll be back by the turn of the year and I'll have extra money in my pocket. By this time next year we will be away.'

He was trying too hard to convince her.

'What if you don't come back?' she asked quietly.

He felt her tears drop onto his hand and held her close. His own eyes were misty now and he could speak no more. He lifted her head and kissed her potently, the flesh of their lips burning with emotion. Then they held each other as the sun slipped away, the breeze rippled the grass and the rocks sat unmoved.

The night of the Road Dance was upon them. In a flurry of preparation Kirsty and Annie fussed over their clothes and brushed each other's hair. Annie asked about Murdo Book. What was he like? And Kirsty had laughed and told her some of it. Sorrow lurked beyond this night but she had resolved to enjoy the time they had left together, and Annie's light mood was infectious.

Kirsty had chosen her best skirt, a heavy, wine-coloured velvet that her mother had brought home from the mainland when she was a young woman. She would wear her white blouse, the one she saved for going to church. And she had a brooch at her throat, a red garnet set in a Celtic tangle of silver. Annie helped her tie up her hair.

Murdo was proud to escort his girl. When he knocked on the door he heard a commotion of muffled squeals and urgent whispers from within, though when the door was opened Kirsty's mother seemed almost serene. He was invited in and sat awkwardly waiting for Kirsty to appear as her mother plied him with questions and small talk. How was his own mother keeping and what a terrible thing this war was. Kirsty's father sat by the fire, smoking his pipe. He had said nothing beyond a self conscious 'Aye' when Murdo entered.

When Kirsty appeared it was as if the roof of the house had been lifted and light had flooded the room. Annie followed just behind, almost stumbling into her sister. She saw how Murdo gazed at Kirsty and longed for the day a man would look at her like that.

'We'll see you there, Annie,' said Kirsty and she headed for the door, inclining her head for Murdo to follow. He mumbled a goodbye, and they were out of the house and into the evening. It held much promise. As they walked onto the road, she looked at him and smiled. The harshness of the afternoon sunlight had eased to a mellow evening glow. Murdo told Kirsty that she looked wonderful.

The lilt of the music could be heard some distance away. As Murdo and Kirsty drew closer, laughter rose to meet them. The Road Dance was not yet in full flow, but some early revellers were getting warmed up. The merry sound of the accordions carried the mood to them. There would be two of them, played by Norman Ruadh and Gee Gee, whose proper name was used by no-one. Kenny John would be there with his fiddle and there would be bagpipes as well.

As Murdo and Kirsty came round the final twist in the road they saw the folk, forty or so of them yarning away in small groups. Their number would easily pass a hundred before long. The Road Dance was held on a straight stretch of road close to the loch side that allowed for large dance sets. Although tonight's had been planned, the Road Dance was normally a spontaneous affair. On a summer evening the local young folk would gather here, one of the central points in the district. Among the laughing and joking a squeezebox would start to play, a lad would proffer an arm to a girl and the dancing would begin.

Tonight's was special, though. Tables had been brought, covered in linen and home baking. Someone had taken a cart into town and come back with barrels of beer and some whisky. The older folk would be there as well. There would be plenty time for solitary contemplation when the boys went off to war, but tonight was a night for everyone, a night of communal merriment. A night when the warmth of shared carousing would help sustain through the cold days to come, when the young blood of the villages trickled away.

Some heads turned when Kirsty and Murdo arrived together.

'Is that Kirsty with Murdo Book?'

'Are they courting?'

Murdo barely controlled the smile of pride pulling at the corners of his mouth. Yes, Kirsty was arriving with Murdo Book. The bonniest girl in the village, and she was arriving with him. Kirsty blushed.

Iain Ban stared hard. He had been watching for her, as he always did. He had seen her walking in the distance and was unsettled by the figure walking with her.

Iain was not in the Militia, but he had seen the excitement around the lads who would be soldiers and he envied them. There was talk of volunteers being needed and he had decided to sign up. Tonight he would tell Kirsty that nothing would make him prouder than if she would consent to being his girl. Time was short.

He focused at the point where the road re-emerged from behind a hillock. Then he could see that it was Murdo Book. The realisation of what it meant only hit home when they came close to the gathering and he could see them holding hands and their smiles and their glances. His heart kicked hard. He had sensed nothing of this. Iain had seen his future around him, the croft, the house he would build, and Kirsty. Now suddenly for the first time there was doubt. It was worse for having it thrust into his face.

For most, though, the sight of the new sweethearts was of momentary interest. Others were arriving and there was much to talk about. The evening was coming alive with chatter and the almost absent-minded accompaniment of the accordions. Louder male voices issued instructions while the tables were put in place. There was laddish laughter as the first of the beer barrels was punctured and giggling from the girls, all turned out in their best clothes. Even the birds seemed to be twittering with anticipation. The sound of the water of the loch lapping the shore was drowned and there was little in the way of a breeze now.

Kirsty looked around at all the familiar faces. There was Dr MacLean, a mainlander who had come to the district some five years previously, a quiet man who had the admiration of his patients. Uisdean the storekeeper was there, Miss MacDonald and Miss Ferguson, the school teachers, and even Mr Hector, the head teacher. An august gathering indeed. The road was daubed with people, and every available bump in the ground was being used as a makeshift seat, as was the drystone dyke on the side of the road opposite the loch. A hundred people, thought Kirsty; yes, and maybe twice that.

Suddenly there was the sound of life being breathed into the bagpipes as the drones sounded out their wail and the piper loosened his fingers by quickly working them through the scale on the chanter. The accordions became as one and the fiddle joined their rhythm. The dance was about to begin.

There was no pronouncement from the players. The dancers would simply recognise the tune and know the dance. Whoops went up as the musicians began a *Strip the Willow*, an energetic whirl of bodies and clapping and foot stamping. Murdo did not even look at Kirsty as he grasped her hand and led her on. They joined three other couples, the women on one side of the road, the men on the other. More groups of four couples formed all the way along the stretch. There was much calling and glancing up and down the line as each set got itself organised. An extra couple needed here, a bit of extra space there, and even as some were still finding their places, the music was away at full tilt, and the dancers with it. Grasping hands, spinning one way, then at the change of beat spinning the other, now linking arms as the girl twirled down the men in the set, each time being returned to her partner in the middle, his arms ready to grasp and spin her again. And after the last man they would whirl for longer until the next phrase of the music, all the time their eyes trying to lock onto something that was not awhirl, before the man would go spinning through the women, mirroring what his partner had just completed. And then they would both repeat what they had just done, in a final dizzying frenzy. As they returned breathless laughing to the end of the line, a second couple was already reeling.

The drive of the music, the crunching of the stones in the road, the hard clapping and the whooping had transformed the gathering within moments from one of promise to one of gaiety, energy and fun. The Road Dance was underway.

A gentler *Gay Gordons* was followed by the *Military Two-Step* which provoked much ironic laughter. More energy in a *Dashing White Sergeant* and an *Eightsome Reel*, the music men gauging the will of the crowd. Bursts of energy followed by an easier mood as the throng regained their breath. Not everyone danced all of the time, but most were scrunching the road at any one note. It was like a village wedding to which everyone had been invited. Mothers and sons, fathers and daughters danced, neighbours reeled, cousins whirled while the older folk watched, blethered and smiled. In the midst, younger children copied their elders. On the fringes lads flushed with adrenalin and alcohol approached the girls and laughed with them, teased and flirted. The girls responded in kind. These were no longer silly boys, tomorrow they would be on their way to be soldiers.

Murdo and Kirsty danced as often as they could, but it would not have been right to ignore the offers from others. Murdo was grabbed for a dance by Kirsty's sister Annie.

'Well Murdo, you're the quiet one,' she laughed. 'Do you want to marry my sister?'

'What did she tell you?' Murdo asked shyly.

'Oh, that you'd promised her a White House bigger than Iain Ban's and that she would have a child a year,' said Annie, deliberately offhand.

'Oh, at least,' grinned Murdo, sweeping her into another twirl.

Iain Ban sought Kirsty for a waltz. He did not say anything, he just touched her shoulder and jerked his head toward the dancing. Kirsty could not deny him a dance, but she was uncomfortable as she followed behind him. He turned to face her and fixed his arms in the dancing pose. She came up to him and he grasped her hand and awkwardly circled the other around her waist. They danced stiffly.

'There's a good turn-out,' she said, in an effort to ease the strain between them.

'Are you with Murdo Book?' he asked sternly, ignoring her question.

'We came to the dance together,' she responded uncomfortably.

'I saw that. That's what I'm asking. You and Murdo Book?'

'Well, we've been seeing each other sometimes.'

'Murdo Book?' His tone verged on contempt.

'Yes. Murdo.'

'You never thought to tell me?'

The arrogance of the question left her speechless. They continued to dance, Iain unsmiling and vigorous and Kirsty going through the motions, wanting the dance to end. He broke the silence again.

'You knew what I had planned, Kirsty. You knew how I felt about you. And yet you couldn't tell me. You couldn't say to me that you wanted to be with him.'

'Iain, that's not fair!' she protested. 'It wasn't something I planned. And anyway, why should I have had to tell you?'

'Why should you have to tell me? You should have told me and you know you should. I've spent my time working to build something that would give you and me a good start together. And while I did that, Murdo big-for-his-boots Book was sneaking in, talking his fancy talk. You should have told me.'

'But Iain. Murdo has done nothing wrong and… I love him.'

'What! You love a man who's good for nothing but his damned books? You just feel sorry for him, don't you? He's going off to the war and you feel sorry for him. That's all it is. You'll see.'

'I gave you no reason to think I would go with you. Whatever you thought, I never gave you reason for it. I never promised anything.'

She knew he liked her and she had been flattered, but knew that she had never led him on. If he had expected more, that was because of his own arrogance rather than anything she had done.

As their exchange became more strident people around them began to notice.

'One day you will see how wrong you are.'

'Iain, I don't want to talk about it any more.'

The waltz was coming to an end. He didn't even thank her at its conclusion, but merely waited until she had turned to go. If he had expected her to say something, he had misread her again. There was nothing she could say.

When Murdo and Kirsty danced together again the intimacy between them grew. Apart from their kisses and his comforting hugs there had been a physical formality between them, unspoken limits. But as they danced he was more aware than he could ever have supposed of her form, the tautness of her body and the swell of her breasts. As they moved forwards and back together he could not take his eyes off her, as she span beneath his upstretched arm her face was alive in the embers of the daylight, her eyes flashing and her hair almost alight. And when they came together to waltz he pulled her tight, closing the rigid inches of decorum between them, and she did not resist. He ached and wanted to hold her within him. What had started for him as a meeting of minds had rapidly and uncontrollably become a helpless love.

It was no less so for Kirsty. She now saw in Murdo a depth that she had begun to explore, and the further she went the more engulfed she became. She had never really noticed his smile before, but tonight he was doing little else. How she wanted to hold his head close so that he smiled just for her, how she wanted to stroke him and kiss him. She felt desire, strong surges of passion that she little understood and that made her tremble. This was the man she wanted to be with, and how she wanted this night to never end. She did not even think of the morning to come because then he would be leaving.

The sun had long gone and the light came from the fire that had been kindled by the loch. It crackled and sparked as the flames danced on the shimmering inky blue of the water. Some now had plenty whisky in their blood, on their breath and in their eyes and the dance was moving to a crescendo after which, on past form, it would fade to overlong farewells.

Over the evening, two paths had become flattened through the heather. Each led to a separate hillock some fifty yards away, behind which calls of nature could be discreetly answered. Kirsty saw that Murdo had been corralled by some friends. The drink had fired their inquisitiveness. This would be an ideal moment to slip away briefly. She smiled as she heard them banter with him.

'How did you manage that then, Murdo?'

'What's she like?' asked another suggestively.

That would be Donald Fraser, or Donald Letch as the women called him. Despite being at least a decade older than most of them he always hung around with the younger ones to talk about women. His conversation was lewd, and yet most suspected he had never even kissed a woman. With the face of a rutting deer, he would ask a lad with a girlfriend how far he'd got and what he'd done. The boys tolerated him because he was older and presented himself as the voice of experience. His drinking tales and stories of women fascinated the uninitiated until they began to realise what a sad figure he really was. Kirsty could not hear how Murdo responded, but she knew by the tone of his voice that it was respectful. She smiled all the more.

A couple of girls passed her on the way back and tittered as they went past. Kirsty knew that other liaisons would be made this night.

As she came round the hillock there was no one else there. When she had relieved herself she began to walk back to the festivities, taking another route round the edge of the loch. This would bring her back into the throng almost unnoticed and she wanted to sneak up on Murdo and surprise him. She heard a movement in the darkness, but thought little of it. Others may be coming to do just as she had done, or it might be a sheep nearby. The sky remained light although the sun was long gone, but the moor was a dark mass against it. The loch was defined by the various specks of light from the fire and the moon sparkling on it, but the land was a scape of indistinct contours and shadows. It held no alarm for Kirsty, this was all so familiar and walking in the dark was nothing new. She was accustomed to the sounds of the night. A closer sound of the brushing of the heather barely registered with her.

There was a dip on the loch bank that took her behind a white rock, the face of which was exposed to the loch, but which on the other side was covered in a thick layer of peat and looked like simply another small knoll on the moorland. The ground rose again just ten feet on. As she carefully stepped down the dip she heard the thudding of heavy steps running behind her. Before she could turn, a force barged against her back driving her against the rock's bluntly serrated surface, banging her head and scraping her face. She gasped in the sweet stench of alcohol. Instinctively, she tried to push herself back but was instantly jammed against the rock. She was too dazed to make sense of what was happening. A hand pushed against the base of her skull, rasping her cheek up the rock and forcing her throat against it. She found herself struggling for breath. Swallowing was impossible. She tried to lever her arms to press her shoulders back, but they were quickly grasped and twisted behind her, a shoulder now clamping her to the crag.

All she could hear was heavy breathing and a rough grunting right next to her ear.

Kirsty's throat was so constricted, only a whimper escaped. She felt her wrists being bound by a belt, the body-weight of her attacker denying her any movement. The belt bit into her wrists. She was now aware of blood trickling down over her eyebrow and down the back of her throat. With her hands now tied, the attacker stood back, using an arm to keep her where she was. With a huge effort she kicked back with her right leg and felt her heel crack against a leg. There was a growl of pain, but even as she tried to yell, the arm pushed her back against the rock and her legs were kicked away from her. Her face tore against the rock's cold flintiness as she slumped to her knees.

The hand moved away from her neck and she felt the shoulder against it again. She frantically wriggled her hands, but they were tied tight and beginning to go numb. She tried to kick her legs back again, but she couldn't muster any force and whoever was there was ready for any resistance now. Then she felt her skirts being lifted and a hand roughly grabbing at her underwear. Now she knew what was happening and the terror surged further. She could not scream and she could not use her hands. She could not kick back. Her only hope now was to resist as fiercely as she could. But he was forcing himself hard against her, overpowering her. She squealed and squirmed, but her head was yanked fiercely back by the hair and thrust against the rock again and again until her pain subsided into oblivion.

It was the burning sensation that stirred her back into consciousness. Between her legs was on fire and inside she was in agony. Although still on her knees, she had fallen to her right side and was in a semi-kneeling, semi-lying position. Her head thumped and her face was beginning to sting through the numbness. She flopped round to sit, and almost screamed with the spasm that shot through her. Her hands hugged her abdomen as she curled forward, pulling her knees towards her head. She could taste the blood in her mouth and feel the swelling on her face, but it was the pain within her that she could not bear, so sharp it cut through the fog in her head. A feather-like trickle between her legs meant she must be bleeding. She could feel that her face was not right and she tremulously touched it, wincing as her fingers traced lumps and cuts. Slowly, thickly she tried to understand what had happened.

3

SHE DID NOT KNOW what time had passed. Adrift in a whirl of confusion and trauma, what had happened was so sudden and shocking in its savagery that it was beyond anything she could understand. When understanding did come, with it came hopelessness and despair. And shame. She felt unclean and unconsciously began trying to scrub herself with her dress, frantically, as if to scrub herself raw. But nothing could take it away. His filth she could feel within, clinging to her insides, cleaving to her mind.

The sound of someone nearby made her stiffen and shake at the same time. Was he coming back? She tried to stand, steadying herself to run, then she heard Murdo's voice softly calling her name.

'Kirsty! Kirsty!'

He had come looking for her.

The only thing that seemed clear was that Murdo could not know and must never know what had happened to her. Through her pain she understood he would be leaving within hours and would be gone for months. There would be nothing he could do to help her, and knowing of what had happened to her would weigh heavily upon him. She feared everything might change if he found out, that perhaps he would be turned off her, would no longer regard her as pure.

Kirsty manoeuvred herself upright, using her arm to balance herself against the rock, feeling it tacky where her shredded face had bled on it. She wanted to curl up, to cry and have Murdo cradle her until the pain went away. Her brain throbbed. Murdo was closer now. With a deep breath she stepped from behind the rock, the effort of it unbalancing her. He was almost upon her now and she stumbled into his arms.

'Kirsty! Are you alright?'

She could not reply, as Murdo lifted her head from his arm he saw her swollen face, gashed and bleeding.

'My God!' he cried. 'What happened?'

She forced herself to speak.

'I fell,' she slurred, hearing her voice sound weak and unconvincing.

'You fell? Where? Where did you fall? Kirsty, speak to me!'

'I fell,' she said more insistently. 'The rock. I banged my head on it. I'm fine.'

'We need to get you to the doctor. Can you walk?'

He put her arm round his neck and supported her round her waist. Her foot scuffed along the ground as she tried to walk and her head fell forward.

There was a struggle going on between her spirit and body. She just wanted to sleep in Murdo's arms, but her head thumped and pain jarred her every movement. Nausea brimmed in her throat. Murdo's voice trying to get her to walk and to speak, seemed distant. She didn't want to speak, only to sleep. She was safe now and couldn't resist the impulse to swoon away. She was toiling to make sense of anything around her. A strange dimness was settling upon her.

Murdo, seeing her wavering on the brink of unconsciousness, was beginning to panic. He crouched slightly, swung his left arm behind her knees and swept her up to carry her.

'Kirsty, don't sleep! Don't sleep! Talk to me.'

She moaned incoherently.

'Keep talking to me. How far did you fall? How far did you fall onto the rock?'

This time there was no sound. She hung limply in his arms. As he stumbled through the gnarled roots of the heather, he was yelling breathlessly at her now.

'Kirsty! Wake up! Talk to me. You're going to be fine. I'm taking you to the doctor.'

She was deaf to his voice, to the straining of his breath and the pounding of his feet.

He was nearing the dance again and yelling for the doctor, but the music had sharpened the spirits and dulled the senses and no one heard. He stumbled his way through a swinging set with Kirsty in his arms. Only the sight of her bloodied face made them grasp that something was wrong. Then there was a commotion and willing hands proffered help.

'What happened?'

'I don't know,' said Murdo desperately. 'Where is he? Where's Dr MacLean?'

He had been at the dance and two lads recklessly thrust through the other revellers calling for him. After some minutes it was clear he had already left.

There was a crowd round where Murdo had lain Kirsty on the grass. Boys at the back with too much liquor jostled forward, thinking they were missing a brawl. It would not have been the first scuffle of the night; Iain Ban, stoked by the whisky, had struck out at Donald Letch in a flash of temper and continued pummelling him until he was hauled off by three bystanders. The incident had gone largely unnoticed, but those near the beer barrels had seen it and an older man had admonished him as he stomped off into the night. Iain Ban's aggression was startling. He had no reputation for alcohol or belligerence. Whatever Donald Letch had said he was regretting it now, holding a handkerchief to his face and slumped bewildered against the dyke. There was little sympathy for him and soon the attention of the witnesses was diverted elsewhere and the Letch had skulked away.

The blood and cuts on Kirsty's face caused gasps of astonishment and a chorus of impulsive questions.

'What happened?'

'Who did that?'

'Get the doctor for the girl.'

Murdo felt the crowd close in on him and started pushing them back.

'Let her have some air,' he yelled. 'Where's the damn doctor?'

'I think he's gone, Murdo. I think he's away home,' someone said.

Cursing, Murdo picked Kirsty up and once again forced his

way through the swarm in the direction of the doctor's house, which lay about half a mile away. A wake of concerned dancers, still flushed from their exertions, followed behind. A gaggle of young boys, excited by the events of the evening and the lateness of the hour, seized the chance to be a part of the rescue and ran ahead to alert Dr MacLean. Some offered to carry Kirsty, but Murdo ignored them and tramped towards the house, finding it easier on the road than it had been through the sod of the moor. Kirsty's head bobbled on his arm, the blood from her face staining his sleeve. The blood from between her legs seeped into her skirts but he was not aware of it.

Dr James MacLean had drunk far, far too much. He'd skipped his way through some jigs and waltzes and, with his wife absent and in her bed and his mood so jolly, he'd fair gulped the drink. He'd even blacked out, couldn't remember leaving the dance and only came back to himself again as he retched violently and repeatedly in the ditch outside his home. His head swirled with voices and noise and light. With disgust, he told himself he was a mess. It was happening again, people would see him for what he really was and he must control it.

Drink was the reason Dr MacLean was on the island at all. At his surgery in the west end of Glasgow he had been establishing a good practice and was well thought of by his patients, who were mostly drawn from the city's genteel set. He was young and attentive and had a sympathetic manner with elderly ladies and their worries. He and his wife found themselves being invited to dinner parties in sandstone mansions where they would listen and nod to the expositions of the city's élite, the industrialists and the merchants, cannily realising that compliant agreement was what they sought.

But for Dr MacLean it was an act that he found increasingly difficult to sustain. His calm air masked a lack of confidence that he could not efface, at least not without his regular crutch, the whisky that acted like soothing oil on the churning acids of his stomach. The amber nectar had been a good friend since student days when annual exams had been a constant anxiety. It had been an unacknowledged mistress, and a generous one, never questioning when he needed more from it. Their assignations were brief, snatched affairs, out of sight of questioning eyes. Estelle, his wife never knew – was, he thought, too dull and naïve to know.

The relationship had lasted for some years before the whisky turned on him. As he aged he traded sympathy for cynicism, and his patients began to notice. Disinterest, and on occasion downright impatience, supplanted the apparently genuine concern that encouraged his patients to confide in him. Now they even began to doubt his diagnoses. But they only began to talk amongst each other when they could smell the whisky on his breath. The word spread. Distrust undermined him, and he fell from favour.

Social invitations became less frequent when nice Dr MacLean became argumentative, upsetting the gentility of these occasions. It climaxed at a dinner when a businessman who was also an elder of the Kirk dismissed the poverty abundant in their great city, pronouncing to general approval that the Lord helped those who helped themselves.

'This city is the engine of the world,' his discourse had continued. 'There is work to be had for anyone who wants it and there is a good life to be made. Too many of these people don't want to work. And when we give them work, they still complain.'

Dr MacLean gazed at his cigar and saw the light a little glazed through his brandy glass. In the golden liquid he seemed to see the faces of the hopeless and the poverty-stricken people he passed on the city's streets, well away from the plenty before them now.

'They complain, sir,' he began suddenly, surprised by the sound of his own voice, 'because of the wages they are paid. They hear of how this city drives the empire and yet they live in homes that breed disease, they cannot feed their families as they would like or afford a doctor when their children get sick.'

'That is balderdash!'

'Is it?' The table was hushed now. Estelle tugged at his sleeve and some ash dropped onto his plate. 'I see it, y'know. I see it everywhere I look. Don't you? You're supposed to be a Christian man. Don't you ever look? Poverty up every close. But these people work, by God they work. Doesn't seem to do much good. They make the engines that drive the empire, but they get nothing back for it. It is no surprise they complain.'

'They are paid what they are worth, sir. If they were paid any more, no one could buy what they make. Then where would they be? They'd know poverty then, believe me.'

'And you know what that means, do you? You know what poverty is?'

The other guests shifted uncomfortably. Arguments of principle were all very well, if inappropriate at the dinner table, but this was becoming personal.

'No, I don't. You're right, I don't. But poverty means to have nothing. The reason so many of them have nothing is because they drink it all away. The pubs are never empty in these parts of town.'

'They drink to escape. Don't you see that?' Dr MacLean persisted.

'They drink because they have the money to drink, then they blame the likes of me who gives them a job for not paying them enough. I've heard your sort of talk before and I'm surprised, frankly. That is the talk of those, what do they call themselves? Labourites. You're one of those damned revolutionaries, sir.' The man's eyes blazed and his ruffled whiskers twitched.

'No. I'm one of those humans,' he responded with pointed emphasis, then sat back and took a last swig from his glass.

There had been a potent silence as the eminent one glared at the doctor, and the doctor gazed languidly back at him with the contented pose of a man who no longer gave a damn. The tension was broken by their hostess, Mrs Fotheringham, instructing the maid to offer more cake.

The end was not long in coming. Perhaps he could have survived the ending of the invitations, perhaps he could have disguised his drinking... perhaps. A confusion with a near-hysterical female patient who had taken news badly hastened his demise. He had not meant to slap her nearly so hard, he'd only meant to calm her, but the sips he had taken from the bottle earlier made him misjudge. His partners told him to go quietly. After more than a year of looking for another practice he realised that the word on him was out. Enthusiasm from potential partners faded quickly after initial, promising discussions. This was the way he had finally come to the islands.

There were not the same comforts here, not the same genteel company, but Dr MacLean came to like it well enough. The people gave him unquestioning respect because he was the doctor, he was educated and he could help them. He kept his drinking until he went home now. It helped blot out his wife, who bitterly resented their change in circumstances and reminded him of it at the slightest opportunity. There were people of her class on the island, but they were in the town, a day's ride away. Here she had the minister's wife for companionship, and that was it. The other women were of no interest to her. This had been brought upon her by her husband and she resented him for it with a vengeance, but having no means of her own she had to remain with him. Tonight, though, she was already in her bed and the doctor could sit with a glass, watch the fire and try to find peace within himself.

The banging on the door stirred him. A young boy was standing there gasping.

'We need your help, Doctor,' he panted. 'A girl's been badly hurt. They're bringing her now.'

The doctor could hear the approaching disturbance. His mind tried to crank up again. He had hoped he could escape the turmoil of it, but the night was refusing to leave him.

'Bring her in.'

Murdo was struggling. He was four hundred yards from the door and his gasps of breath seemed to be delivering less and less oxygen to his straining muscles. He focused on the light but he didn't seem to be getting any closer.

'Walk with her, Murdo, walk. You might be hurting her more with the running,' someone said.

It made sense. He wanted to run, to get her there quickly, but he understood that in his desperation to do right by her, perhaps he was harming her. As he slowed to a fast walk, her head rested more easily against his arm. He couldn't tell how she was breathing, but he could feel the heat between them and the sweat was dripping down his body. He whispered reassurances to her and at last he was stumbling through the doctor's doorway. Only now was he willing to relinquish her.

Even then there was doubt. The doctor looked bleary and unkempt and smelled of drink. He was now at the front door, leaning heavily against the frame telling the crowd that they must go, there was nothing more they could do. A jacket lay outside, stained and stinking. The doctor slammed the door shut and stood momentarily with his hands pressed against it and his head sunk between his shoulders, exhaling loudly, whether in exhaustion or to regain composure Murdo could not tell. He had to remind himself that the doctor could do more for Kirsty than he could.

A lamp glowed on the stairs and a shrill voice called down. Dr MacLean barked back irritably, 'It's a patient.' Nothing more was heard from upstairs.

'Bring her through here and lay her on the couch,' the doctor instructed Murdo. His head was beginning to clear.

'She fell,' Murdo began to explain as he lowered her gently.

'I'll see to her,' said the doctor, easing him aside. 'You've done what you could. You go home now.'

'I don't want to leave her,' said Murdo.

The doctor said nothing for a moment as he gently moved Kirsty's head with his fingers, examining the gashes on her face.

'Very well,' he said flatly. 'You can sleep in the outhouse. My wife. You understand. Go now. I'll take care of Kirsty.'

'Thank you,' said Murdo, hovering momentarily before leaving.

Lights and sounds burst through Kirsty's head as she surfaced to consciousness and she was seized by a severe pain between her legs. Her mind reeled in a confusion of nightmare impressions. She felt somebody near and opened her eyes. Her pupils shrunk from the brightness of a fire and she closed her eyes again. She opened them again, tentatively, and saw a silhouetted figure sitting by her.

'How are you feeling, Kirsty?' a voice asked gently. 'It's Dr MacLean. You're in my house.'

Kirsty didn't speak and her eyes filled with tears.

'Take your time,' the doctor said reassuringly.

Incoherent thoughts whirled in a murky confusion of images and torment. She was sick and sore. Her head was swathed in bandages and she could smell disinfectant. She gazed at the ceiling. She was lying on a couch in a strange room. The doctor sat facing her in an upright chair close to her head. A fire was burning in the fireplace. The doctor was holding a glass in his hand. She heard him swallow deeply and then the chair creaked as he leaned forward.

'Do you remember what happened, Kirsty?' he asked quietly.

The smell of the whisky on his breath instantly took her back to the awful moments of her rape. Her back arched and she whimpered.

'Kirsty. Do you remember what happened?'

She was living it again, the terror, the pain, the helplessness. She groaned and cried aloud, feeling her skin stretch and pull where she'd been bandaged. He placed his hand on her shoulder in a hopelessly inadequate gesture of compassion. At length she relapsed into a frozen quiescence. She might have confided in the doctor, this man who had sat as her protector, cleansed her wounds and tried to ease her dejection. But she knew she must not. That way, only she and her attacker would know, and neither could tell.

Dr MacLean gave her a handkerchief and she dabbed her eyes. She must tell him something because she would not be left to her silence.

'I remember running,' she began hesitantly. 'Round by the rock at the lochside. I tripped. I must have banged my head against it. I don't really know.'

The doctor's intent face was very close to her now, leaning urgently forward with his elbows on his knees and his whisky glass clutched in both hands. The flickering fire light caught in his eyes and she could see a wet slick of the whisky on his lips.

'Are you quite sure?' he breathed. 'Nothing else happened?'

A tear rolled down her face and her lips contorted as she tried to stop herself crying aloud again. The room was very warm and her body hurt. She wondered if Dr MacLean somehow knew.

'That was all,' she finally answered, as strongly as she could.

Dr MacLean continued to look at her. The fire threw his shadow swollen and flickering on the wall behind him. Silence hung heavily, punctured only by the ticking of a grandfather clock and the sparking of the burning peat. Suddenly he sat back, startling her.

'Good,' he said. 'Good.' And took another gulp from his glass.

'You see if you can get some more sleep and I'll arrange for you to be taken home when the daylight comes.'

'Did Murdo bring me here?' she asked, her voice steadier.

'Yes he did. He carried you all the way. He didn't want to leave you, either.'

'Did he?'

'He's asleep in the outhouse. He'll take you home.'

Kirsty began feeling faint again and as she lay her head back and let her eyes close, Dr MacLean watched over her.

When next she stirred it was Murdo who was with her, leaning over gazing at her face. The touch of his breath had wakened her. He barely brushed her lips with a kiss.

'It's time to get you home,' he whispered.

The room was lighter, but colder. Daylight had come. She could see it force itself through the weave of the curtain fabric. The fire was dead, and the grate piled with grey ash. Dr MacLean was asleep in the chair, his head slumped onto his shoulder and his jaw locked open. An empty glass sat on the floor beside him. There was something in his form that made Kirsty sad for him, something forlorn and pitiable.

Murdo threw back the blanket that covered her. Kirsty moved her legs to the floor and stopped suddenly as she felt something pressing against her crotch.

'Put your weight on me,' Murdo reassured her, slipping her arm around his shoulder and pulling her to her feet. 'The doctor says you'll be fine.'

Kirsty wasn't listening to him. The unfamiliar pressure between legs was tormenting her.

'Could you leave me for a moment?' she almost snapped.

'Leave?' She could hear the hurt in his voice.

'I need to sort myself,' she said more gently.

Murdo left the room and she instantly hitched her skirts. A bandage had been folded into a pad and placed inside her pants to stem the blood that had flowed earlier. Only Dr MacLean could have done that. He had known something else had happened, but he hadn't forced her to say. She felt a well of affection for the slumbering figure and padded over to him to gently kiss his forehead.

Murdo was waiting in the hall.

'Shouldn't we tell the doctor we're away?' he asked.

'He's been awake most of the night watching me. We'll leave him to sleep.'

The doctor slept on as they left the house. The room was cold in the early morning, but no colder than his bed would have been next to his wife.

The previous night one of the boys had told Murdo he would bring along a horse and cart to take Kirsty home. He had been as good as his word. Murdo guided her slowly over to the cart and lifted her on to it. She was so weak that she would have been unable to do so herself. Her head was a constant shank of pain. And worse, she felt as though there were a jagged stick inside her, invading her and defiling her. She sat silently as Murdo brought the horse over to hitch it up. The animal snorted and a plume of hot breath billowed around it. Its hooves clumped on the grass verge and then clopped on the stones of the road. Kirsty breathed in the fresh air of the morning. A hint of peat smoke infiltrated it. The cold air caused her to shiver and the pain in her head to intensify, but once that had passed she felt better for it.

The grey, dawn mist was fading as the sun rose higher. Birds chirruped excitedly. It was going to be a wonderful day, a day of colour and glory. A day for young men to go off to war.

She watched Murdo as he pulled on straps and buckles and stroked the horse's head and she felt a foreboding in her soul. How she loved this man, and yet so much had changed since they came together only days before. Everything was so grim now. She could never be the same woman again after the vile attack, and today he was leaving. The certainty of those wonderful first hours was now a mass of doubts. Would he ever come back to her? If he did, would she be there for him? She feared the ragged pain inside her and did not dare imagine what its consequences might be. The dread of it all made her want to cry out. Instead, she silently implored the Lord to spare them both.

At last he was beside her, pulling himself onto the cart. She wrapped her arms round his and rested her head on his shoulder as he grasped the reins and flicked the horse onto the road home. The jolt made her wince, but he would be with her for the next precious few hours, and that was all that mattered.

They said almost nothing on that journey. How could they without ever saying he would be leaving? For the short time remaining they could be lost in each other without having to confront the inevitable.

As the cart trundled up to Kirsty's house, Murdo kissed her gently on the head. 'The boys are leaving in two hours. I'll go to the house and get my things and I'll meet you back at the gate.'

Her mother and sister dashed out to her and her father stood watching from the doorway. Her mother had been awake all night. How was she, the poor soul? She must get into the house and lie down. What had the doctor said? Amid the clucking and fussing Kirsty heard the cart rattle away, and despite the concern from her family she wished she was with Murdo.

Murdo's mother stood at the door of their home. Her lips were set unnaturally firm, but the flaring nostrils and the tears in her eyes betrayed her. They had agreed she would not go with him to the lochside. Their parting would be a private one. A hug, a kiss on her flushed cheek as she sniffed back the tears and a simple goodbye was all either could bear.

She tried to tell him to write, but the words wouldn't come. She could only nod. As he walked away with his younger brothers, he turned every few yards to raise a wave to the figure in the doorway of home. As he watched her bravely holding her hand high, flapping a farewell with her fingers, he felt the swell of tears in his own eyes. All he had thought of these past days had been had been leaving Kirsty. This painful parting from his mother had stolen up on him unawares. How sore it was. Kirsty had so filled his spirit, but his mother was so much part of him. That he had almost overlooked her in those dramatic last hours pierced him with guilt. What for her now? They had drawn strength from each other.

As he reached the corner that would finally wrest him from her sight, he gave one last wave, pulled the handles of bag onto his shoulder and was gone. His mother stepped back behind the door. Now at last she could weep for the boy who'd had to grow so quickly on the death of his father and who was now going off to war. How bitter life could be to those so good.

Murdo's brothers walked along quietly, aware of his heavy heart. They had been stirred by the glamour and only now did the thought of the sorrow it could bring creep into their minds. When Murdo asked them to run ahead to the lochside, it was a release.

Kirsty had taken off the swathes of bandage, determined not to say farewell looking so absurd. Now her hair hung free in its rich glory, veiling the injuries to her face.

His head was down and she could only see his cap and the white of the shirt and scarf he wore beneath a dark Harris Tweed jacket. He was transformed from the man of the early morning. It would take everything she had to buoy his spirits. She would have to be strong. She walked to him and slipped her hand into his.

'So this is it,' he sighed.

'Only for now,' she said.

'I shouldn't have to do this. Kirsty, I don't care what's happening in Europe. It's nothing to do with me. Our future is America and I'm being tied down by a history that's not even mine.'

Kirsty walked with him, letting him unburden himself to her. But the chance was quickly denied him. As they walked village folk came to their doors to wish him well. He had to let go of Kirsty's hand as the men grasped his and shook it firmly. They would pray for him, they said. And Murdo knew that if God listened to prayers then he would be alright. These were genuine people, good people, and they would respectfully ask the Lord to look after the boys. If sincerity of faith and power of belief had any effect, Murdo knew that the Lord would look after him on the battlefield. There was little jingoism. Sending their young men off to war had been a sad ritual for so long for the people of the island, and the dust of many of these boys blew across the historic battlefields of Europe and beyond. Yet again the King had called from so far away, and again the young bloods had rallied to the cry. And when the steel had clashed and the guns had roared and the victory had been won, those who were left would return home to be forgotten again. The islanders knew this and yet they always marched. It was God's will, some said.

Murdo looked upon the familiar faces, faces that he'd known all his life, and it saddened him to be leaving them. Some old women slipped him small parcels. 'For the journey, my dear.'

'If leaving is as hard as this now, what will it be like when I leave for America?'

Kirsty let him talk.

'All I've thought about for years is getting to America. I suppose I knew it would mean leaving my mother and the family, but I've never really confronted that. Maybe I didn't allow myself to. My mother always told me she never said goodbye to my father when he left for the fishing, because then he would come back. She never did say goodbye to him and after he was lost, how that has tormented her. But when I go to America, I'll be saying farewell to her, knowing I'll never see her again. How can I do that?'

'Don't you want to any more?' Kirsty asked after a pause.

'Cutting my ties with the past won't be difficult. But turning my back on my present? That will be so hard.'

Twelve hours before, the scene at the lochside had been so different. There was no music this time, only subdued voices and a universal heaviness of spirit that could almost be seen. It showed in the tear-stained faces of the mothers and sisters who had come to see the lads off and in the strained looks of fathers and sons. The minister was there too, with his dark clothes, his black Bible and his overcast face.

Murdo was the last to arrive. Ten young men stood ready to walk off to war. This was the worst time. When they set off they would provide mutual support and they would look forward to the adventures ahead. Before that, though, came the send off and the farewells.

The Reverend MacIver stepped forward, flanked by the elders of the church. He bowed his head, paused until everyone had followed his lead and began to pray. He thanked the Lord for

His Goodness and begged forgiveness for their sins. He spoke in a monotone and even as he struggled to find his words, his voice filled the gaps in the flow with a tonal moan. As he pronounced that the fate of these brave boys was in the hands of the Lord, he swayed gently back and forward, his face set in a grimace. If it was God's Will, he intoned, that any of these boys should not return, pray let them fear none ill as they walked through Death's dark vale. For twenty minutes he prayed, oblivious to the tears that were seeping again among his congregation.

Reverend MacIver wasn't finished there. He flicked through the light leafs of his Bible until he settled upon Mark, Chapter 10. His voice was tremulous now.

'Jesus said, 'I tell you this: there is no one who has given up home, brothers or sisters, mother, father or children, or land, for my sake and for the Gospel, who will not receive in this age a hundred times as much…"

He led the singing of Psalm 23 himself and pronounced one last prayer. Then the minister approached each of the young men and shook them firmly by the hand.

Murdo turned away and clasped the heads of his two brothers to his chest. They fought not to sob. Murdo, as so often since his father had died, found the strength he needed to comfort them.

'You be good for Mam,' he instructed. 'You know what needs doing. Now it's up to you to see to it. You have to be men now. D'you understand?'

The boys nodded, their lips trembling.

Calum Boer approached.

'Your mother will not be on her own, lad, have no fear of that.'

'That's good of you, Calum.'

The older man took his arm and led him to one side.

'I've been there Murdo. I know something of what's waiting for you. I'm not telling you to scare you, but I know you're a sensible lad and I want you to be prepared. You will see death, and death on the battlefield is a cursed sight. Forget glory. Remember the people you are fighting for are waiting for you back here. There is not much victory for them if you don't return. Do your duty, lad. That'll make you a hero enough. And don't worry about home.

Your mother will be fine.'

They shook hands firmly, the older man gripping Murdo's elbow.

'Say your goodbyes.'

Similar scenes of embrace and parting were being played out along the lochside. It was a sombre dance, with woman embracing men, except the women were all older and their faces were seared with sadness. Final gazes were made at faces they had known so intimately from the cradle. Bold young men off to war they may be, but they were still their children. Final farewells were made and after the tearful embrace, a clasping of hands in a last bonding before the off.

Murdo was with Kirsty and the tears were in his eyes. It made her realise how little she knew this man who filled her heart. Despite her own tears and the anticipation that he would be sorrowful, the reality of it weakened her, although her voice remained strong.

'I'll be here waiting for you, my love. And America will be waiting for us both.'

He embraced her and hugged her so hard that she would have struggled for breath had he held her too long. He pulled his head back and gazed at her before kissing her. His lips were so soft as the blood swept to his face and she could feel the heat of his emotion. As she closed her eyes the tears ran to their mouths and although she could faintly taste the salt, it was the sweetest of kisses.   When they separated, the other soldier boys were already gathering together at the moor road, ready to walk the miles to town. Murdo picked up his bag, already a red tinge to his eyes the only sign of his sorrow. The bagpipes sounded a march. The ten young men set off together to a rousing three cheers. Some of the men threw their caps in the air. They watched as their sons, brothers and sweethearts walked up the incline of the moor road, turned for a final wave before their heads bobbed out of sight down the other side. It was the last some of them ever saw of their loved ones and for those who watched them go that final cheery wave was carved in their memory.

Kirsty stood watching, staring at the point where the top of the brae met the sky. There, moments before, Murdo had looked round for a final glimpse of her, still near enough for her to run after him, still close enough to hear her call. And yet he was gone and she didn't know when he would return. She could not let herself think that she might not see him again.

The crowd began to disperse, drifting back to homes that would seem emptier. For Kirsty the pain from her ordeal of the previous night began to return. She had subconsciously held it at bay until Murdo had gone and now it came back to her, forcing the air from. An older woman saw her and misunderstood.

'It's always painful, my dear, but you be strong for him.'

Kirsty eased herself onto a boulder to sit. The woman put a soothing arm round her shoulders, unaware of the extent of Kirsty's anguish. She so desperately wanted to be alone. And yet she had never felt so lonely.

4

THE ROCK MADE HER MOVE. She had not wanted to leave the road where she and Murdo had danced together. Perhaps the longer she waited the longer the spirit of that night would linger around her. Every step towards home would take her further away from him. She stared bleakly at the hill, knowing he was on the other side walking on the stony road to town. She could still see him if she ran to the top of the brae, but she didn't. They had said goodbye and it would be even harder to watch him walking away from her. She wanted to stay where she was, but the presence of the rock brooding over her and the memories it brought, she could not bear.

Most of its mass was hidden where the peat and the heather swelled over it, but at one side the white-flecked grey of the gneiss rose too sharply for any earth to cling to it. When she looked over her shoulder she could see it, could feel its flinty sharpness tearing through her flesh as her head was rammed against it. Her hand involuntarily shot to her cheek. She had to get away from the rock's incriminating stare.

Others were making their way back to homes that would be sadder places. Wives held their husbands' arms, fathers walked with faces stoic and grim, mothers dabbed handkerchiefs to red eyes amid sniffs and sobs. It was a straggling funeral cortege for boys who still lived.

Kirsty rose and began her own solitary walk, trying to preserve images of Murdo in her mind's eye, but her thoughts of him were constantly jabbed by pain. She was still clotting and she felt torn inside. When she had walked with Murdo to the lochside earlier her willpower had overcome the physical pain. Now, with him gone, there was nothing to distract her from her wounds.

And there was a fear, a dread she must now confront.

Could she be carrying the beginnings of a child?

Could it be that the seed of the devil who had overcome her could be causing a baby to grow within her?

Was that the cause of the agony she was feeling in her body? She did not know exactly how a child was created in the womb, but she had tended enough animals to know the physical action required. That was how her attacker had treated her, like a beast to be served, only worse. It repelled her to think that she might give birth to a baby brought to her in this way. A child should be a yield of love, the sort of love she had for Murdo. If she were pregnant then what would this one be?

The other awful question was who had done this to her. The thought struck her forcefully. Someone she knew had done unspeakable things to her. Maybe there had been a stranger hiding out of sight, but the whisky on his breath suggested to her it was someone who had been at the dance. Had she danced with him, laughed with him? Could he have been at the farewell? She glanced around in fear that he might be nearby. Was he watching her now? There was an animal in him and she dreaded that he might be unleashed again.

The thought of Mary Horseshoe loomed before her. If she was pregnant, who would believe that she was a victim? She could hear Old Peggy now, harshly telling people that she'd been warned often enough. 'Interfered with was she? We've only got her word for it. You can't expect to put temptation in front of young lads at the dancing when they're fired up by the drink and the devil.' Even worse, what if they thought it was Murdo's baby? That's what they would all say. How could she tell her mother? How could she tell Murdo, now so far away? How could she love a child that had been forced upon her, a child that would be her's, but not Murdo's?

She was lost in her torment. As she passed the church, she didn't notice a figure emerging from beside the wall. The man checked the road in both directions before advancing hastily towards her. As he came to her she heard the sound of his boots and became aware that she was not on her own. She span round in alarm.

'Kirsty,' he called.

She saw that it was Dr MacLean.

*

He hadn't known what time it was when he finally woke. It had been an uncomfortable introduction to a new day, but not one he was unused to. The first sensation had been a dull, persistent ache in his head. The dry tissue of his throat stuck together as he instinctively swallowed, forcing a rush of bile into the sluice gate of his gullet. He jolted upright. The sudden motion made his head spin and he felt his neck crick as the muscles abruptly pulled out of their constriction. He clasped his hands to his face and hung his head again. His breath came in pants and he swallowed each time he inhaled as he tried to control his stomach. The chill in the room made him shiver. There was always a payback when he returned to reality from the drink. The suffering was always the same. At least he had been here often enough before to know it would pass once he had got fluids into his system. He began to make his unsteady way to the kitchen. Then he saw the blanket folded on the couch and the events of the earlier hours flashed back. He looked around, but she had gone. In the kitchen he slurped from a milk jug, the shaking of his hands spilling white trails down his chin. He leaned on the table, bracing himself in case it came straight back up again. When it didn't, he began to place peats slowly into the stove. Once he got the fire going and brewed up some tea he would feel better.

He remembered Kirsty being in the house, because the condition she was in had sobered him somewhat. The events leading up to her arrival, though, were obscured out of any coherent sequence. Her head had been a bloody mess. The wounds were superficial, mostly to her forehead and down one side of her face: two gashes, some grazing and bruising. A tooth looked to have been chipped and her tongue cut.

As he had worked on her the blur of the alcohol had cleared. What disturbed him most was how, even though she was drifting in and out of consciousness, she held her hands protectively over her groin. While she was unconscious he gently moved her arms away and rucked up her skirt. A cursory examination confirmed that she had been subjected to rough intercourse. He had to swallow

69

hard. He'd cleaned her as best he could and left a dressing in place. Having made her as comfortable as possible, he had taken his whisky bottle from the shelf and poured a tumblerful to ease the shake in his hands. Then he'd sat and watched over her and wept pitifully.

She had stirred some time later and they had spoken, but little had come from it before she fell asleep again. He hadn't remembered falling asleep in the armchair and he'd heard nothing of her leaving.

He knew he must speak to her, but it would have to be a private conversation. For the meantime a drink would help him think everything through.

'I didn't mean to scare you, Kirsty. I just wanted to see how you were. How is your head?'

She touched the cotton on her cheek and managed a weak smile.

'You should have rested.'

She couldn't respond.

'I had to check on you,' Dr MacLean said by way of explanation. 'I knew you'd have come to see the boys off and I knew I would see you here. You should be at home resting.'

'I'm going home now,' she said almost in a whisper.

As she began walking again he fell in beside her. She didn't want to look at him, knowing it wasn't just the wounds to her head that concerned the doctor. He knew what injuries she had there, and he had come to find out more. She didn't want to tell him anything.

They walked a few yards in silence. There was the wind and the crunch of the stones on the road and the distant sound of the sea and the gurgle of the river, but they were so familiar, so much part of living here, that it seemed that the silence was total. When he spoke the doctor's mild tones could not have seemed sharper to Kirsty.

'Kirsty, what happened? What really happened? Can you tell me?'

Kirsty pressed her chin into her breastbone and unconsciously began to walk faster to escape Dr MacLean's probing and the sight of the rock and the horror of its memory. But he grasped her arm to stop her and as he did so her face crumpled in tears.

'Kirsty,' he said softly to try to soothe her. 'Kirsty, no one else need know what happened, but I have to know that you are alright. You know that I know. You don't need to tell me anything you don't want to, but you must come to me if there are problems.'

Dr MacLean looked a tired man, not from lack of sleep, but from exhaustion of spirit. Bags weighed down his eyes and the lines did not hint at laughter. His thinning hair lacked life and lustre and although there was no weight in his face it seemed to sag in chronic defeat. But the concern in his voice reached out to Kirsty and she felt her words leak away from her.

'How could someone do that?' she asked through tears. 'How could someone hurt me like that?'

The doctor helped her over to a dyke and leaned her against it. She was quivering, her fists forced against her eyes. He bowed his head and sighed deeply before speaking, all the while keeping his hand steady on her arm.

'Who knows what demons drive people, Kirsty? And God knows, these demons will be all the greater today. I can't protect you from that. All I can do is try to help you.'

'What can you do?' she asked, her helplessness ripped by a rising rage. 'He's ruined me. He's dirtied me. What can you do about that?'

The doctor stood and said nothing.

'Oh, you could help me where I'm torn, but you can't help what he's done to me here,' she said clasping her hands and thudding them against her chest. The force of her anger broke on the final words and she sobbed once more.

Dr MacLean offered her a crumpled handkerchief and moved round to sit beside her on the dyke. Kirsty struggled to contain herself, forcing the handkerchief against her eyes, her tremulous breathing causing it to flap. The doctor remained motionless, his head bowed, his hands clasped between his legs and his forearms resting on his thighs.

'He's destroyed me, doctor,' she whispered.

'You mustn't let yourself think that. He hasn't destroyed you.

You've been hurt in a way that's unforgivable, but don't let it destroy you. Don't think like that. You weren't to blame. You did nothing wrong, you've no cause to feel ashamed. I can't tell you how to feel, but your life didn't end last night. Your mind will heal too. It all takes time.'

'But I'll never be able to forget it, doctor, how can I?'

'I don't mean that you should. But you must try to leave it behind you. Don't carry it with you. That's what would destroy you.'

Kirsty tried to absorb what the doctor had said while he tried to convince himself that it was true.

'Doctor,' Kirsty began hesitantly, 'do you think he could have made me expect a baby?'

Dr MacLean breathed in.

'It's possible, Kirsty. It is possible.'

The confirmation barely seemed to penetrate. She sat with her hands clasped on her lap, looking down at the handkerchief she still held.

'We will know in time. What matters now is that you get the proper care you need. I will come and see you.'

Kirsty gripped his arm, and her eyes, though swollen and red, lost their dead expression and came alive with urgency.

'No. Don't do that. If I need you I'll come to you. No one must ever know what happened to me,' she said fiercely. 'You mustn't tell anyone.'

'I can't tell anyone, Kirsty.'

They parted.

The talk with the doctor had given her hope. It was only possible she might be pregnant, so she might not be. She would cling to that hope and pray for it. Yet even as she resolved to do so, she questioned why she should pray.

This was a cruel life that let her glimpse what could be, then wrenched it from her, as it tore her body and took her love away. Was all this made to happen by a God who loved her? Why so much misery, she wanted to ask Him? Why did He allow so much crying, so much despair? These were simple questions, she knew, and the greater mind of the minister and the unshakeable faith of her mother would have answers. But Kirsty, in the depths of her anguish, doubted for the first time that their explanations could satisfy her.

This community had suffered tragedy more than most. Death hovered in the wind; it rode the waves that smashed the rocks and seeped through the earth to ruin the crops. It stalked the young and the old. Its visits were accepted with a fortitude built on the faith that each soul would find peace at the feet of the Lord for time everlasting. Beyond the sorrow there was the solace that a loved one went on to a better place. Death could be spoken of as part of life. Death, whenever and however it arrived, was accepted.

The creation of life was different. There was joy of course, but it was not the event of death. Then the silence would hang heavy. There was not the corresponding community elation when a child was born. Village life would continue as on any other day. Visitors would come with gifts and wish the new baby well on its journey through life, but as the fate of Mary Horseshoe's daughter made clear, it was not an unquestioning acceptance. Mutterings would cling to a child born less than the full term after its parents' marriage, and that fact would remain with it throughout its days. The gossips would never lose sight of the fact that the child's parents had had to get married. It was only after Mary Early had had three premature births that it was accepted that she had been justified in wearing white on her wedding day. Calum an Lochan had been born eight months after his parents' marriage, the reason, according to Old Peggy, why he was such a wild child. Death was held in greater reverence than birth, and perhaps even than life itself. The premature loss of a child – a tragically common event – would bring more attention bustling to a house than the birth immediately preceding it.

As she walked home, Kirsty forced her mind to dwell on the places that had become so special to her and Murdo in the short time they were together: the twist in the road where they had first come upon the Road Dance, the spot on the moor where their love had blossomed, and even from here she could see the ocean, barely audible this far inland but alive in colour and motion and possibility. The sea might not be the only barrier to their hopes now. And always she would think of him on the moor road to town. Would he be laughing with the other boys, would he be thinking of her? She felt he was.

The way home took her past Old Peggy's house and inevitably conversation with her. Old Peggy would sit outside her door, spinning at her wheel, clacking her knitting needles together or simply watching, missing nothing. Nobody walked by her door uninterrupted. Her conversation was inquisitorial. How was the family? What were you doing? All the while she was gathering threads and weaving them together making a fabric of village life. She felt herself to be the communal conscience, the arbiter of what was morally right. In her own judgement, she herself had led a good life and had faced her misfortunes steadfastly. Her cupboards were bare of bones. She had not missed a day in church since her days of childbirth. Not a funeral service took place without Old Peggy being there, sitting upright at the front of the mourners, her hands resting on her walking stick. It was this righteousness that allowed her to observe and comment on the lives of others. It was a privilege she took seriously. She knew everyone and knew their history, and what she didn't know, she supposed.

Kirsty could hear the click, click, clicking of the needles as she approached the grey stone of Old Peggy's house. Despite the trauma of her rape, the fear of pregnancy and the emptiness left by Murdo's departure, there was further for her heart to fall. Old Peggy would know something had happened, she may not know exactly what, but she would know something and she would want to know more. She could prise what she wanted from you. Kirsty would need to be sharp and strong to keep her secret and she didn't feel she could be.

Click, click, click, 'Hello, Kirsty', click, click, click. The voice cracked through the bustle of the needles.

'Are you alright, girl?' she asked without waiting for a reply, 'Look at your poor face. It's a terrible thing to happen on the night before the boys leave. And your head, girl, what happened to your head? The drink, my girl, that's what it is. The drink drives men to the devil.'

It was a tactic of Old Peggy's to bombard her victim with

a barrage of questions and statements, to pummel them into a response. And when they denied or confirmed, she would have them, they would be talking.

'What they did to you was terrible.'

Kirsty panicked. What did she know? If Old Peggy knew, soon enough everyone would know. The clicking of the needles demanded a response.

'No one did anything to me. I fell.'

'Are you okay, girl?'

'Yes thank you. I just got a bang on my head.' Kirsty worried that maybe she had sounded too defensive.

'I hear you stayed the night at the doctor's, my dear. It must have been a terrible thump you took. Surely you weren't touching the drink yourself, girl?'

Old Peggy chuckled. This was her idea of teasing.

'No I wasn't. I just fell. I tripped and fell. Nobody else was near me.'

'Were you running, girl? You have to be careful on the moor. You must have fallen with some force to hurt yourself like that.'

Kirsty hesitated. She would have to lie, but Old Peggy was wily. She would pounce on any inconsistency like a cat on a mouse.

'Yes, I was running.'

The old woman smiled revealing the stumps of her remaining teeth. She winked suggestively.

'One of the boys chasing you, girl?'

'No. I was hurrying back to the dance. I really need to get home now.'

'Of course, my dear.'

Old Peggy knew she was lying. She would find out soon enough what was behind all this. She had one more trick to play and as Kirsty turned to go she asked quietly, 'Has Constable MacRae seen you yet? He was asking if I'd seen you.'

Kirsty swayed and swallowed. Old Peggy had hit home, and she knew it.

'Oh yes, you'll need to see the police about it,' she said with quiet satisfaction. 'You'd better get home girl, you really don't look well. If I see the officer, I'll tell him I saw you.'

If she could Kirsty would have run, just run and run. Instead, she could only limp away. Not for a moment had she even thought of the police. Why would the police get involved? What had they been told? Police. Questions and answers. Everything was running out of control. They would be getting involved in what she had wanted to keep to her most private self. The physical rape had might be over, but the emotional rape would be equally brutal and it would go on. She had been attacked, she had been raped and that could not be swept away, even if she wanted to. What her attacker had done to her, he could do to others. The police would want to know exactly, in detail, what had occurred. Word would get out. How did they know?

She didn't know how she summoned the strength to complete the last part of her journey to her home near the shore. She shuffled along, every step a conscious effort, and every few houses she had to withstand further conversations. She was caught in a disorientating vortex of questions and civilities.

'Are the boys away?'

'Brave lads that they are, brave lads.

'Of course you'll miss him, my dear.'

'They'll be back soon enough.'

'Your face girl, how did that happen?'

Finally she was home, her legs almost numb and her head too. Her mother was waiting for her, expecting to hear how well the boys looked as they walked off, wanting to know who had all been there. But Kirsty mumbled that she was tired and stumbled past, through to the bedroom. Mam came right in behind her.

'Kirsty, are you alright?'

'I'm just tired Mam, I'm so tired.'

'You've been trying to do too much,' Mam chided. 'You should never have gone so far. Will I send your brother for the doctor?'

With the last of her energy, Kirsty managed an emphatic 'No!' Mam helped her undress. She climbed between the sheets and sleep swept her away.

It took only an hour for him to come. For an hour she huddled in her bed, her sleep disturbed as her mind and body relived the trauma of what she had endured. She woke panting and sweating.

This was no bad dream that would fade when she came to and she lay tossing from one side to another. Slowly her breathing calmed and her panic subsided.

She hadn't fallen asleep again, but there was some sense of protection cocooned in the dark. Then she heard the scrape of the policeman's boots on the stones of the path, the curt rap on the door and his authoritative voice greeting her mother and asking if she was home. Her heart began pounding again.

Constable John MacRae was well respected and liked. There was little crime to be solved. His role was more one of keeping the peace, the occasional row over the ownership of an animal or a piece of land, or more likely a drunk with a loud mouth and aggressive manner. He lived near the church and his children went to the village school. There was a delicate line between being a member of the community and his position as official arbitrator. It was a help that he was not local so he was not immersed in some of the family tensions that developed over the years. Nonetheless, he was from the islands and had an understanding of the people and their ways. He tried to settle disputes without resorting to the court in the town. He had lived here for five years and what he had been told of the previous night's incident made it potentially the most serious problem he'd faced.

Old Peggy had been at his door that morning. A girl had been injured at the Road Dance, she'd told him, and what else could be expected when such debauchery was allowed? She said she didn't know what had happened and it was none of her business anyway, but the girl had spent the night at Dr MacLean's, and that couldn't be right. Old Peggy had just thought he ought to know.

MacRae couldn't pretend to like the old woman, but she was a useful source of information and he had often been able to defuse a problem before it had come to anything because of snippets she had told him.

He had spoken to Dr MacLean and had been surprised by the doctor's reticence. The two men had dealings with each other from time to time and had a cordial enough relationship. But the doctor had been defensive, apparently surprised to see him and telling him that there was really nothing the police need get involved in. From what he could glean, though, Kirsty's injuries were more than might have been expected from a fall. John MacRae was curious.

'Kirsty,' her mother said urgently. 'Constable MacRae is here to see you.'

Kirsty lay curled, hugging the sheets between her legs and chest. Her breathing suggested that she was awake and as her mother grew accustomed to the dark she could see the glint of her daughter's eyes. Her instinct was to hold her daughter, to cradle her through her suffering. But the police were at the house and the police were authority and that could not be questioned.

'Constable MacRae just wants to ask you about your fall,' she said. 'Why don't you come out and see him?'

Kirsty lay without moving. She did not know what he would ask, she did not know what he knew. Her mother had accepted the story that she had fallen and banged her head. There had been no reason for her to think otherwise.

'Tell him to come through,' she murmured.

Her mother left her, pausing only to pull open the single curtain strung across the small skylight cut into the thatched roof. Moments later she heard the metal studs of the policeman's boots clattering on the stone floor of the house. The wooden door that separated the sleeping quarters from the living room scraped open and there he stood. He seemed to fill the room. Kirsty pulled herself into a sitting position, her back against the wall and the sheets pulled up to her neck. It was an involuntary, defensive movement and PC MacRae saw it. His curiosity grew. He knew Kirsty as a bright, friendly girl. Why was she so scared?

'Hello Kirsty. How are you feeling?'

There was a long pause, too long a pause for an innocuous question.

'Better, thank you.'

'Your mother tells me you were seeing the lads away. Let's hope they'll be back soon.'

She nodded her head slightly.

'Dr MacLean seems to think you should have stayed in your bed.'

This time there was no pause, and a sharpness in her voice.

'What did he say to you?'

'Nothing, Kirsty, nothing. He just told me you'd got a bang on the head and he thought you'd been concussed and he'd have been happier if you'd stayed at home.'

'It's a bang on the head, that's all. I wanted to see the boys off.'

'Uh huh.'

The silence returned. The policeman gazed steadily at the girl and she stared back at him before dropping her head slightly and glancing about the floor.

'That was all, Kirsty? You fell and hit your head off the rock? No one was chasing you or carrying on?'

'No,' she said, almost irritably. 'There was no one near me.'

'If there is anything more, Kirsty, you should tell me. If someone did this to you, tell me.'

'There's nothing more to tell,' she said with all the force she had left.

'Okay, Kirsty. I'll leave you be. If you think of anything else you want to say, you know where I am.'

She didn't look at him as he stood up. The figure sitting on the chair with his hat off, talking gently to her, and looking at her kindly might have teased more from her over a longer period of time. But now that he stood, so tall, he was once again authority and the tenderness he had shown her as he sat speaking to her was lost. The policeman observed that she was still not looking at him. He knew she was lying, but without her co-operation he could do nothing. Who was she protecting? As he stooped to go through the doorway into the living room, he spoke over his shoulder.

'I hope I don't hear of anyone else having an accident like this, Kirsty.'

He instantly disliked himself. The girl was wounded and sore and that must have sounded like a threat. She did not deserve that.

Behind the closed door, Kirsty remained hunched in her bed, sobbing silently, all defiance exhausted.

Her gloom only lifted when the photograph came. The letter was addressed to her, the first she'd ever had in her life. She knew it was from Murdo, although she had never seen his handwriting before; that momentary thought of how little she knew of her love made her sniff back a tear. The writing was a flowing script. The envelope was thicker than any other she had seen delivered to the house. Annie and her mother stood watching her expectantly. Normally mail was addressed to her father and the family would watch as he carefully slit the envelope open with a knife and read through the contents slowly and silently before sharing the news with them. But Kirsty wanted to be on her own. She could already feel her heart racing and she did not know how she would react when she started to read Murdo's words. She went outside, round the end of the house. Annie tried to follow, but Mam understood and kept her back.

The postmark showed the letter had been sent from Glasgow. He was already so far away. She slit the corner with the edge of a cracked seashell that had been dropped by a passing gull, thrust her finger inside and along the crease, anxious to open it as delicately as she could. Four sheets of paper were folded neatly in half and as she slipped them out of the envelope she could feel something hard inside them. The unexpected sight of his face made her heart turn over.

The sepia print was on a stiff cardboard postcard. There he stood uniformed, upright and somehow different. There was a solemnity about him that she did not recognise. Some might have thought it was pride, but she knew he did not want to be where he was wearing what he was. His tunic was buttoned to his neck and she worried that it might chafe him. She had never seen him wear a kilt and the plain khaki apron over the one he wore in the picture took the life away from it. He held his cap in one hand, the other resting on the back of a stout, wooden chair. His mouth was set firm and his hair combed tight. She'd known him those few days as a man who could bring the world to life through his words and laughter, a man whose wavy hair was tossed by the wind. The photograph did not show such a man, but it was unmistakeably his features and she knew she would treasure it and keep it with her to feel closer to him. The back of the card was split into two sections, one for correspondence and one for an address. A line of small print separated them, giving the name of the photographer in Glasgow where the picture had been taken. He had written on the back, 'To my love and my future.' She kissed his image, careful that her tears did not stain it.

'My Darling,' the letter began. 'My Darling'. He didn't use her name because he didn't need to; she was his darling, his one and his only, and through her tears that brought joy to her.

My Darling,

I miss you so much already. I have been away not one month yet, but each day I miss you more and I wonder how long I can go without seeing you again. They say we'll be back by Christmas and that cheers the other lads because they think it is not so long. I think it has been too long already and waiting for Christmas fills me with dread. I feel as if I had just begun to live and it was taken away from me so soon. I want to live again and it is you who breathes life into me. I will just have to be strong.

How are you? I was so worried after you hurt your head, but the doctor told me you would be fine. It was a dreadful thing to happen, but I hope you have got over it.

We are in Glasgow on our way to a camp in the South. From there we will be crossing the water to whatever fate awaits us. The lads are excited about it. They want to get at the Germans with their bayonets. I don't ask them why. I don't think they would even know.

I hope you like the photograph. I have sent one to my mother also. I have never seen myself like that before because I have never had my photograph taken. It is a strange experience. I am sure there will be a lot of new experiences over the next few months.

There is a good crowd of lads with me, including the boys who left the village with me. Iain a' Bhuth is saying that the army is such a good life that even when it is all over he will be staying on to become a regular. I think having us all together has helped us settle in, although there is not much chance to settle anywhere because we are being moved on so quickly. For some of the boys it is not quickly enough. It is hard work and we are training all the time and although it helps the time to pass you are never far from my mind.

One of the boys has been writing a song about home. Calum Morrison has shown me some of the verses and it is a beautiful song. He is missing home as much as me and his words are full of praise for the island and the village. I miss home, but not the land, as he does. I miss the people and I miss you more than anyone.

I don't want to finish writing this because there has been so much I wanted to say and to tell you. I feel as if each time I put pencil to paper I am speaking to you and I can see you listening to me and for a few moments I am back with you.

Alas, my darling, I must send this letter off now. We are moving on again. My next letter might come from France and how fancy that will be.

With all my love,
Murdo.

Kirsty pored over his words, oblivious to everything around her. She read each paragraph over again and could almost hear his voice. She was torn between joy and desolation. He had told her she was the breath of his life, that she was his 'darling'. She had his photograph to carry with her and to look at when the loneliness became too much. However the letter also told her how melancholy her love was and while that reassured her in a way she did not like, it compounded her own despondency. Tenderly she kissed his image once again and lost herself in melancholy longing, for how long she did not know.

5

FOR TWO MONTHS she did not bleed. It had been the first time since that frightening but ultimately thrilling day when her mother told her she was no longer a girl, but a young woman.

Kirsty told herself that it was because of the shock. She tried to keep it from her mind and sometimes if she was busy or involved, she could forget. But always the uncertainty came back to her and she felt her heart and stomach mash together. Each morning in the days before she was due to menstruate she would sleep fitfully and waken feeling tense because no blood had come. She tried to convince herself that it was the worry that was upsetting her system.

The only real relief was the further letters from Murdo. Each one a thrill, each one replenishing her with his words and his love. As soon as she finished one, she longed for another, wanting to know so much of what he was doing. The only way she could be part of it was to read them over and over again. Each night she kissed his image. Every time she received a letter she sat that night to write him one by return, reciprocating his love. She wrote so freely. What she could say on paper was more than she would be able to say when they were actually together. She told him what was happening in the village and any stories she heard from those over in America. She took to knitting, and Mam did too, sending him socks and mittens. She and Annie talked of going to town to get a photograph taken to send to him. The letters were so good for her, lightening her spirits for a while and making her feel close to him. But always reality would settle upon her once more.

The third month she knew. Days after she had expected the blood to start, there was still none. Her body was changing: her breasts increasingly tender and a tightness in her lower abdomen. She knew now that it had not been nerves that had made her sick on those two or three occasions. Kirsty was expecting her rapist's baby.

The awful import of what was growing inside her pushed her into a darkness in her soul, to a place she had never been before. She did not know that she had fallen there. She was in a constant panic, she could not eat, could not converse. Her mind was gnawed by this awful truth. Her fear was dragging her into the darker quarters of her being, pits in her psyche that she did not even know were there. All she was conscious of was agitation and dread. This was no open sore that could be balmed. This was a growth within, a tumour that would destroy her life as surely as if it was a cancer.

For days she endured this anguish. She told her concerned mother that she was having a difficult time of the month and Mam had accepted that readily. The bruises from the attack had faded from sight and from the front of Mam's mind. She made no connection. Slowly, Kirsty appeared to emerge from the gloom and she did so on the back of the realisation that she had to. She saw that it was not the baby growing inside her that would ruin her, but people's knowledge of it. If they did not know, they would have no reason to treat her any differently. That would give her time, to do what, she did not know, but at least she could think.

People still saw the same Kirsty. They saw no change; they did not hear a baby squealing beneath her skirt, there were no tiny hands jerkily grasping at the air, there was no swaddled figure suckling from her. There was not even a swelling. Then they would notice. That would have them pointing and condemning. But, on the outside at least, Kirsty was the same as ever, physically at least: the tall, slim girl with the flashing eyes and untamed mane of hair. Those who were close to her may have noticed a slipping of spirit, but she had a ready answer.

'Are you alright Kirsty?' Annie had asked one night as they lay in bed. Annie was disturbed by her sister's restlessness.

'Yes.'

'You've not been yourself. You've been so down.'

'I'm fine,' Kirsty said, forcing a smile into her voice.

Kirsty had thought long and hard about this situation and had known that the first person she would have to talk to would be Annie. They had always been close, despite being very different both in personality and in appearance. Kirsty was vivacious where Annie was withdrawn and sensible, the sort of girl of whom Old Peggy approved. She was always a steadying influence for Kirsty. Annie did not resent her sister's good looks or popularity with the boys, indeed, she was occasionally embarrassed for Kirsty if she felt she was being too flighty. They cared for each other and they looked after each other and shared everything. But Kirsty could not bring herself to tell Annie what she was struggling so hard to accept herself.

'I miss Murdo,' she told her sister. 'I know I haven't told you much about it. I suppose I was scared that you would tell me I was letting myself go too quickly. I think I love him. No, I know that I love him. It's the first time I've ever felt like this, Annie. But he's been taken away from me and I'm left feeling empty.'

Annie lay, listening intently. She knew that Murdo and Kirsty were courting, but this depth of feeling was unexpected. And Kirsty spoke on, in a calculated attempt to deceive her sister, the one person in whom she had always had faith and trust. But faith and trust were strangers to her now because she felt betrayed by them.

'There's something else, Annie,' she whispered, conscious of her sister tensing beside her.

'We were planning to go to America.'

She felt Annie's head twist round to face her.

'America!'

'Yes. We had it all planned. Murdo has saved some money and we were going to stay with his uncle in New York.'

'New York!'

'Shhh! You'll waken Neil.'

'New York,' Annie repeated in an urgent whisper.

'Yes. Murdo was going to get a job with his uncle. I was going to get a job somewhere and we were going to stay there.'

'Oh, Kirsty!'

'I know, I know. But now he's away at the war and I might never see him again. I just miss him so much.'

Kirsty began weeping. Annie turned to her and put an arm

on her shoulder.

'He'll be fine. They're saying they'll be home by Christmas. And maybe it's not such a bad thing that he's away. It'd be a big thing to leave home and it's better that you really think all this through. Maybe the war is God's way of giving you time to be sure that it's what you want to do.'

Kirsty's weeping was not an act. As she spoke she saw her hopes before her again in all their glory and she was back with Murdo on the croft, basking in the glow of the setting sun. Bitterly, but silently, she was scornful of her sister's suggestion that the war was part of God's scheme. She loved her sister and knew she had been trying to comfort her, but the absurdity of the notion exasperated her. Then almost immediately she felt guilty at feeling so dismissive of someone whose only motive had been compassion.

The two women, so close by blood and yet so disparate in mind, lay side by side, the arm of one wrapped around the other, trying to offer comfort, but in the knowledge that she was doing so in vain and could do no more.

The Post Office, ever busy, was the feeding point for news from the Front. The latest despatches would be written on a telegram and put in the window. Simply dated and titled 'Official War News', the postman's neat writing detailed every barrage, every costly retreat, as intimated by the War Office. In the early weeks of the war it had seemed as if the British troops were always retreating. The word 'losses' meant little then, but in the months and years to come they would cause a heaviness in the heart. Place-names from far away became part of everyday conversation: some easily and uniformly pronounced, others repeated in various ways, but understood every time. Mons, Verdun, Ypres, Loos, Neuve Chappelle became part of the village dialogue, little towns in Belgium and Northern France at the centre of the maelstrom that was engulfing all their lives, even here on the edge of the world.

OFFICIAL WAR NEWS
FIGHTING AT THE RIVER MARNE. GERMANS DRIVEN BACK TO

AISNE. FOUR TRAWLERS LOST IN NORTH SEA TO ENEMY MINES.
EASTERN FRONT, RUSSIANS DEFEATED AT TANNEBERG. PETROGRAD
ACKNOWLEDGES 'SEVERE LOSSES'.

These staccato reports were a tenuous, impersonal link they had with their loved ones. The letters from the front came through irregularly, sometimes two or three arriving together. There could never be any knowing the grim reality behind the bald facts, not until after the soft young men had aged and hardened in spirit and soul and returned from the killing for the last time. The sparse, formal lines in the Post Office window said nothing and when the lads wrote home they said nothing either, not only because of the official censorship; they censored themselves. What good would it be to tell their mothers and fathers of the hell they were in? The church warned of eternal damnation for the unbelievers, but they believed, and what could be worse than the deaths they saw. No sad passing on a deathbed here, with death gently holding the breath and guiding it away. Here death leapt upon you and thrust its grasping fingers deep into your chest, ripping, tearing and gouging the life from you. This was no walk in death's dark vale; this desperate dodging of death through the sucking, gorging mud. Here you doubted that God was with you. How could they tell their people that? They sought solace among their comrades and tried to be strong for their loved ones.

Autumn chilled into the wind and the grey and the wet of winter. Each day Kirsty would walk the mile or so to the Post Office, which was housed in a cramped extension to the postman's own home. It could be several days before the message was changed, but when it did Kirsty wanted to see it and feel closer to her Murdo. Even if there was no message there was still the possibility of a letter from Murdo. Peter the Post would see her approaching and would have any letter ready for her.

'The boys are moving north now,' he would say. 'They're not far from the coast. Once they're back at the coast it's just a boat ride home.'

There was no sense of defeat in the news that the lads were retreating. As stories spread of large numbers being killed, there was just a strong desire to have the boys home.

There came more stories of men dying and boats being sunk, with hundreds being lost. The initial excitement felt about the war began to dissipate. Life on the crofts was constant work and whilst thoughts were with those away from home, the work had to continue. It was a life dictated by the weather and when the sun shone you made the most of it. There was little time to dwell on uncertainty. Women busied themselves responding to Queen Mary's call for three hundred thousand pairs of socks to be knitted for the troops.

Iain Ban came to see her. He came right up to the door and asked if he could see her. Mam had invited him in, but when he saw that Annie, Neil and her father were also at home, he asked Kirsty if he could speak to her alone. Reluctantly she had walked out with him. They had not spoken to each other since the night of the Road Dance. It was only at the church that they ever came across each other, and there he avoided even looking at her. She had become used to that behaviour and, if truth be told, it was a complication less in her life. Now he was here. Outside the door he began heading towards the shore.

'What is it, Iain?'

'I want to talk to you alone. There are things I need to say.'

She stopped.

'Iain. Nothing's changed. What is there to say?'

He turned and beckoned her towards him.

'Please Kirsty, just come with me. Listen to me. Please.'

She walked towards him uncertainly.

'Kirsty, I've joined up. I'm going off to the war.'

He let her absorb his news.

'Well, good, Iain, if that's what you want to do.'

'I've had time to think Kirsty. What I said to you at the dance was unfair, I know that. I shouldn't have said it. I suppose I was hurt at seeing you and Murdo. I'd always thought that it'd be you and me. And I know you never said it, but I just thought that's how it would be. It's how I dreamed it would always be. I spent all my time getting the new house built, and I lost sight of you. That's my fault, and I'm sorry for it.'

They were standing on the rim of the bay, the rocks and pebbles falling before them down to the shoreline. Iain stood looking back up the track to the village, facing her, his back to the sea.

'You've nothing to be sorry for, Iain.'

'There is. I was so angry at you, Kirsty and I thought bad things. I've tortured myself over you.'

He had picked up two small stones and was playing them through his fingers. She watched him intently, wondering what he was leading up to.

'I've thought that maybe if I'd made an effort, things would be different between us.'

He waited for her to speak, tumbling the stones in his hand, his blonde hair blowing over his forehead. He was unable to look straight at her. He could not bear the rejection he might find there. Kirsty knew she would see hurt in his eyes and she looked out to the horizon so she might avoid it.

'Don't torture yourself, Iain. It wouldn't have made any difference. I don't understand how these things are, but you can't choose the people you fall in love with.'

'I don't believe that. You can be made to love someone. They can make you love them. If they show love to you, it is difficult not to give it back. That's the mistake I made. Murdo is not the man for you, he just got there first.'

'I don't want to hear this, Iain, I've told you that before.'

'That's not why I brought you here. It's not what I wanted to say, but it's true.'

'I need to get back,' said Kirsty impatiently.

'I just wanted to tell you that I'm going and that I'm sorry.'

'Iain, there's nothing to be sorry for.'

Kirsty started to make her way away from the shore. He looked so dejected she felt a wave of sympathy for him.

'Come on, Iain. Walk back up with me.'

He cast the stones aside and strode after her.

'What will you do with the house while you're away?' she asked.

'I don't care about the house,' he said. 'It's of no interest to me anymore.'

She turned to look at his downcast face.

'You take care, Iain Ban,' she said kindly.

He touched her arm.

'Think well of me, Kirsty.'

Then he was gone. As she watched him walk away up the road, she worried for him and the gloom around him. She wondered whether she would ever see him again. Then she shivered and went back into the house.

Calum Morrison was on the roof of his house, renewing the thatch, spreading straw over the clods of heather turf that sat on the roof timbers. An old fishing net lay at one end ready to be spread over the straw to keep it in place. It was hard work and usually a job for two men and more. But today Calum worked alone.

Peter the Post was cycling to the house. He had a bad feeling. Over the years he had become familiar with the mail; the postmarks from far-flung places, the unbending envelope that told of a photograph inside, the typewritten address that always indicated official business. He knew the village and the people and he knew more than most about what was happening in their lives. He never liked telegrams. Telegrams either carried news of the birth of a grandchild away in the city, or they told of death. Peter knew that the Morrisons were not expecting a new generation to be added to their family just yet. Calum was their eldest and he was at the war. He had been anxious ever since that day six months ago when he'd taken the batches of buff envelopes round the district calling the young lads to battle. The telegram had been brought over from town that lunchtime, and as soon as he saw it Peter had felt cold.

He made straight for the Morrisons' house. However much he did not want to be the bearer of bad news, that was his duty. Delay would not spare them. He tried to calm himself into believing that it was really nothing serious, but it was a telegram and what else could it say?

He pedalled quickly and a few folk noticed that Peter was in such a hurry he didn't have time for his usual chat. There was warmth in the early spring sunshine and he began to perspire beneath his Royal Mail cap. From about four hundred yards away he could see Calum working away on the thatch. He was a good man, Calum, quiet and dependable. Some years previously he had suffered severe injuries when a fishing smack struck the pier as the boats were being tied up in preparation for an incoming storm, jamming Calum between the boat and the stone of the pier and damaging his left shoulder and hip. He had been bedridden for weeks, a difficult predicament for a man with a young family to support. The community had come together to help but it was too much for a proud man to rely on charity. He did not look down on those who needed community support, but he had felt demeaned while he had to rely on it himself. He had recovered and resumed an independent life. But Peter the Post could see now that Calum was ageing, was stiffer moving about the roof, was slower lifting the thatch from the ground.

'Hello Calum. How are you doing?' said Peter, more brightly than he felt.

Calum looked down, wiping the sweat from his head with his forearm.

'Ah, good Peter, good. And yourself?'

'Aye, fine, fine. That's a power of work you're doing.'

'Ach well, Peter, it's taking me a bit longer y'know, but it still needs doing. Young Calum was helping me last year and we got it down quickly.'

He began to come down from the wall of the blackhouse, more glad of the break than he would care to admit.

'So have you got anything for us there?'

'Aye Calum, I do.'

The postman reached into his bag and lifted out the envelope.

'This came over from town,' he said handing the small brown telegram to Calum.

'Oh! What can this be? Are they wanting the girls to go and fight now eh?' He walked to the doorway and called to his wife.

'Morag, bring me my glasses.' He looked at Peter and winked with a smile. 'We've got a telegram.'

Peter remained rooted where he was, gripping the handlebars

and saddle of his bike, the weight of doom holding him where he was. He did not know what was in that envelope, but everything told him that it was bad, very bad. He heard Calum's wife coming through the house. He had never seen Morag Morrison without a good-natured smile on her face.

'What's all this fuss you're making?' she admonished her husband. 'Hello Peter, and how are you? What d'you make of this fool shouting to all that the King has written us? Now what's this you're talking about, you clown?'

Calum ripped it open and pulled the wire-rimmed glasses over one ear, across the bridge of his nose and over the other ear, blinking his eyes to focus. He held the telegram at arm's length and leaned back, his top lip stretching as he peered. Peter the Post delivered many telegrams after that, too many, and he never again stood to watch them being opened.

'And how's Marion?' asked Morag. 'I was speaking to her at the church last Sabbath and she was saying that her hip was sore.'

Peter wasn't listening. He was staring at Calum as he slowly read, painstakingly mouthing words of a language that was not his first tongue.

'Maybe it'll be better with the dry weather,' went on Morag.

Calum was blinking no more, his eyes were staring hard at the paper and he'd stopped breathing.

'Oh it's painful, is the rheumatism,' continued Morag.

Suddenly Calum slumped back against the wall of the house.

'Oh dear Lord!' he groaned.

'Calum! What? What is it?' In that same instant Morag knew. 'Oh no, not Calum, not my baby.'

She grasped the letter from him, but the English meant nothing to her. She could read the Bible in the Gaelic, but for her English was a language of a few isolated words. These thin strips of ticker-tape stuck to the telegram sheet were indecipherable to her, but she knew their meaning as clearly as if her son had fallen in front of her.

'Oh not Calum.' She crouched to the ground, her head slowly lifting back, her mouth twisting in an agony beyond sound.

Peter clamped his lips together to stop himself sobbing

aloud. Everything stilled and the three formed a tableau of total desolation, the bereft couple unable to reach beyond their own wretchedness to comfort each other. The casual slaughter of a young man in a fleeting moment of battle had its full resonance here in a faraway, peaceful village where it shattered a mother's heart like no shell ever could.

The mother's wailing followed Peter as he walked back home, wheeling his bike beside him. Peter's face was set grim and he cast his eyes unblinking to the road. Those who saw him knew the news had been bad.

From that day on, Peter the Post never delivered a telegram other than with his regular mail. The sight of him cycling through the village with his hat on in the afternoon would have meant only one thing. Even as it was, everyone knew some home might be torn asunder by the envelope he carried. They might breathe easy once passed them by, and then feel guilt because that meant someone else would be in mourning soon. Peter hated his role. He almost began to hate himself. He became as feared as the Grim Reaper himself. The prospect of delivering a telegram filled him with an implacable dread. He would make his leaden way to a home wakening in the morning light, knowing that he would be leaving it in a deep, deep darkness.

Kirsty shuddered when she heard of the death of Calum, the songster Murdo had told her had written a paean to the village and land he loved and to which he would now never return. She had known Calum all her days and was shocked by his death. His passing drove home the harsh realisation that Murdo, too, may never return. She had wept often at the thought that he might not, but now her tears dried up. This was the cold realisation that her beloved Murdo could die.

Life was delivering a series of brutal truths. Christmas had passed, and the war should have ended and brought Murdo back to her. But it had not. As the time trudged forward, Kirsty felt the baby within her grow and move. That first fluttering had not brought a maternal thrill, but was fuel to her fear and forced her to confront again that she was trapped and that the physical release of childbirth would offer no escape. Her height still allowed her to disguise her pregnancy, but that surely could not last long. Annie must notice. They slept in the same bed. How long could Annie fail to see her sister's swelling belly? Sleep, once a deep rest for Kirsty, became fitful. She found herself waking in the very early hours, turbulence in her head and anxiety in her heart. She would worry about Murdo, she would check that she was turned away from Annie. If her sister's arm should stray onto her in her sleep, she would move it away. Annie hadn't noticed because she was not looking and because any small changes in Kirsty were so gradual that she didn't see them as changes at all, but there would soon come a time when there could be no hiding at all.

And now death had taken one of the village boys and the naïve excitement of the late summer of the previous year was gone. The longer it dragged on the more would die. Murdo's latest letter from the Front told her that he was feeling the same way. This letter was different, devoid of optimism and making no attempt at cheerfulness. Its tone was bleak and sour. She was not the only one confronting harsh realities.

My Darling,

I hope you are well and your mother, father and family also.

Things are desolate for us just now. I'm sure you will already have heard what happened to Calum. Dear Calum with his songs and his poetry. His words made us think fondly of home and his singing was a great comfort to us. His passing makes us ever more aware of what fate could await us.

We had been waiting all day to attack, but for some reason it was nearly dark before we went. I can't tell you what that does to your mind. You think you are prepared for what is to come and then there is a delay. You try not to let doubt eat at you, but of course it does. For most of us it was our first taste of real battle. There have been skirmishes but this was full-blooded war. I admit I was scared, we all were, but you are there with your comrades and you try to be strong for each other. You don't want them to see you have the wind up.

You are never away from my mind, my love, but sometimes I am filled with a deep sadness. When I think of the times we had together I feel good, but then I think I might not see you again and I dread that. I know I have never said that to you before, my darling, but now I have seen what could be and we must steel ourselves for it. I had never heard of Neuve Chappelle and neither had Calum, but that is where he died. I have written to his parents, but what can I say? Truth is another victim of this awful affair.

There is little movement here now. The Germans and ourselves are dug in trenches stretching across the north of France into Belgium. No one knows what will happen now or what we'll be doing. Forgive my gloom, my darling, but we are all so low. We lost other lads as well as Calum and it has made us all feel bad. However, if I keep thinking of you and what lies ahead for us together I will be fine.

Take care of yourself my love. I shall write again soon.

With all my love,

Murdo.

Kirsty folded the letter. It was the first she had not re-read immediately. It pulled her down even further. She knew that Murdo was desperately unhappy where he was, but he had always made the effort to make light of it in his letters home. This one was written under no such pretence. If he let such desolation show through, what did that say about what he truly felt?

The sea rolled gently against the shoreline. A fulmar petrel flew up into the sky before turning, as if shot, and dropping like a stone beneath the waves. Kirsty saw in that simple act a parallel with her own life: soaring so high, then plummeting down. At least the petrel had done so of its own choosing and may have a fish in its mouth as a reward. If Kirsty could believe that when she emerged back into the sweet air she too would be better off, then she could cope. But her mind was a tangle of doubt from which she couldn't free herself.

She could never remember how the final weeks passed, how she stopped living a life and instead trudged through each day. She could not recall a single thought from those days. She did the work required of her, ate little, slept less and less. There was increasing discomfort from the sheet she had torn into strips and wrapped tightly around her. It reduced the swell, but breathing was difficult. Her mother told her she was filling out, but no one else noticed. She took to going to her bed before Annie and getting up before her, so that her sister would not see her undressed or in her night-clothes, but that was an instinctive ploy, not something that she rationally thought through.

Springtime was busy for the crofters with planting, peat cutting and lambing. Kirsty took full part, but by the end of the day she could not recall what she had been doing. Only one episode remained with her. One evening her father called her to the byre at the end of the house. A ewe was having trouble delivering its lamb.

'Can you help me here, Kirsty?' he asked in his matter-of-fact way. It was nothing she had not done before, but Kirsty began to tremble, hoping her father wouldn't see as he busied himself with the sheep. She almost bolted, but stopped herself.

'I think the cord is tangled round the lamb's neck,' her father said. 'I'll hold her and you pull out the head and see if you can loosen it.'

His daughter's face was so pallid she looked as though she was about to pass out, but his back was to her as she pressed her hand against the cold stone wall to steady herself. The sheep was writhing and groaning with a deep-throated rattle. Its eyes bulged.

'Come on, come on,' her father urged. 'We can't lose this one.'

Kirsty knelt beside the animal. The lamb's head was already protruding, but while normally the rest of its body would have slid out quickly, it seemed to be stuck fast. The skin of its mother was stretched tight. Kirsty stared in horror.

'Come on! Hurry up!'

Kirsty cleared the mucus from the lamb's nose and mouth and it bleated pathetically. This made the ewe thrash her legs in panic. Kirsty's father edged round to use his side to hold her still. Kirsty then began working her fingers into the birth canal and felt the umbilical cord coiled round the lamb's throat. It wasn't so tight that she couldn't slip her fingers underneath it, but it was constricting more with every squirm of the mother.

'Can it come out?' her father asked urgently.

Kirsty didn't answer. Her hands were now both inserted in the sheep almost up to the knuckles and the flesh would split were she to push any further. She saw her father's eyes looking over his shoulder at her, his mouth hidden by his shoulder. He was looking anxiously at her, glancing sharply at the head of the lamb, and back to her. She couldn't see the sheep's head, but she could hear it snort and feel it jerk. The lamb's head was so black and slippery in her hands and there was urgency in the air. The atmosphere closed in around her; the panting of her father, the rasping of the ewe, the heat in the byre, the warm smells of unfamiliar fluids and somewhere she the screaming of a baby and she saw herself standing above herself pulling a baby's head from her body.

'What's the matter? Pull it out!' she heard her father shout.

She breathed in deeply, closed her eyes and pulled at the head of the lamb. She could feel the neck stretch, the sheep kick and then the lamb slipped out of from the warmth of its mother and flopped, steaming, in a slimy heap of vernix. The placenta followed in moments, along with the rest of the cord.

Kirsty's father released the ewe, which heaved itself onto its legs and immediately went to its newborn. Kirsty walked slowly out of the byre and back up to the house. Her father watched her go before setting about cleaning the lamb. The following day he was involved in organising the fishing and the incident was gone from his mind.

The experience had traumatised Kirsty, who crept into her bed and lay there shuddering. This was what lay ahead of her. Now the certainty of what she must endure within days had been shown to her in all its gore. And she would have to bear it alone.

In the days that followed she confronted the lambing again and again. Her father and brother left for the fishing and on the Western Front Murdo and his comrades first heard of Aubers Ridge.

Before the month was out, Peter the Post held more telegrams his hand.

6

'KIRSTY, THERE'S SOMEONE here for you.'

Mam's voice called from the living room. It was raining heavily and with all the hard work of recent days, Kirsty was taking a rest. Her mental and emotional turmoil was constant, but she could ease her corporal weariness.

She was alert enough to be surprised. Tying her robe loosely about her, she felt a chill run through her as she put her feet on the cold of the stone flooring. Opening the door through to the living quarters she saw Mam looking perplexed.

'It's young Alasdair Morrison. He's at the door, but he won't come in.'

Kirsty's heart lost its rhythm momentarily. Her brain skipped, as if jinking over stones in a burn, making no more than glancing contact with any particular base of thought. Why should Murdo's brother be at the door? What's happened? Oh God, what's happened? Already she had pushed past her mother and was at the door.

The boy's head was bowed. The rain behind him fell in unbroken greys threads unravelling from the slate grey clouds. He was without a jacket and sheltered under the lintel, his shoulders hunched and his hands gripping the sleeves of his woollen jumper. Kirsty could hear Mam behind her.

'Bring the boy in. He's soaked.'

Alasdair looked up as soon as he saw Kirsty appear through the gloom of the house. Although the movement had been sudden, Kirsty saw it in heightened slow motion, feeling every detail as they each jabbed her eyes. The hair clamped close to his head, forming thick cords bound by water. He was shivering, but now that her feet were used to the floor, she knew it wasn't cold. His face tilted towards her and she saw the red swollen eyes and saw his tears mingling with the rain to run down his face. His mouth was half open and his lower lip hung thickly. He was trying to speak, but he could not. And he need not. Kirsty knew.

'Oh, not Murdo!' she cried. 'Not Murdo.'

The boy looked pathetically at her. She grasped his shoulders and gasped.

'Is he just wounded?'

Alasdair could not meet her frantic eyes.

'Oh, God no! Oh God no!'

Mam checked herself from admonishing the blasphemy as she, too, began to understand. Her daughter was screaming and she ran to embrace her. Murdo's brother's expression transformed from abject sorrow to fear.

'Run home to your mother, Alasdair,' Mam commanded, 'She'll be needing you.'

The boy turned and ran, splashing through the puddles as he made for the road. He didn't know for sure why he was running. He would only be returning to a similar scene at home, where his mother was slumped in a chair. He had heard her howling worse than a wounded dog and had dashed in from the byre to find her leaning on the old wooden dresser, indistinctly repeating Murdo's name, over and over again, in a wailing sob.

His other brother had gone to get their aunt, who lived three crofts away. The family had been without their father for a long time and the boys had all learned self-reliance, but this was beyond anything they had confronted before.

Their mother had become like an animal; she had sunk to her knees and had pulled Alasdair to her, clamping her fingers to his side as if she were adrift in a treacherous sea and he was all that held her away from oblivion. Her head was thrust back and her eyes screwed tight as if to cut out the harshness of life's light. Her mouth was now trying to speak, to give some release to her misery, but she could say nothing.

The boy had stood above her, trembling and helpless. He became transfixed by the spittle on her chin and the string of saliva that stretched from her top to bottom lip, barely shivering because no air was being sucked into her mouth.

In one hand there was a crumpled bit of paper and young Alasdair understood. He clasped his mother's head and held her to him, trying to console her in the innocent way of a child.

'Mammy. Mammy. Eeesht Mammy. It'll be alright Mammy, it'll be alright.'

And as he said that, he knew it would never be alright, and his nostrils flared, his eyes blurred and his voice broke away.

His sister, two years older than him and two years younger than Murdo, came running in. She had known from the sound that her big brother would not be returning. She collapsed on the floor with her mother, wrapping her arms around her. The five-year-old baby of the family stood in the doorway from the bedroom confused, frozen by fear and crying hard because her mammy was crying.

In his helplessness Alasdair had sought to escape. The sorrow in the house was suffocating him and like a cornered rabbit he panicked and ran outside, just as his brother Kenny arrived with their aunt, her face white and hollow. She tried to reach to him but he pushed past. He needed to keep moving, it was as if stopping would engulf him. His hero brother, his idol, was dead, but he wasn't even sure what that meant. What was it to die? His brother was lost to him, that he knew, but what did it really mean? His father had died five years ago, shortly before his youngest sister had been born, but he could remember little other than the sorrow of that time. His father was a dim figure to him now, resurrected by his mother only in fond memory or admonishment. Was that what it was to be with Murdo? Was the tragedy of that time to be played out again once more? Was Murdo really dead? Was there a chance that a mistake had been made? Murdo couldn't die.

The boy could not understand. All he did know was that he was agitated and distraught and needed to do something to calm himself, to cleanse the awful truth from his mind. That was when he thought of Kirsty. Somebody would have to tell her. She was Murdo's girl. It fixed his mind to have a task to do. So he raced up the road to her home, tears that he couldn't control streaming down his face.

Now he was hurtling back again, shocked by the impact of

his arrival at Kirsty's, concentrating on his running, eyes fixed firmly to the ground trying not to think of what might greet him. But now his jumper was flapping about him, sodden from the cloudburst, his breeches were chafing sore against his thighs and his feet were nipping from rubbing against the hard leather of his shoes. The rain was stinging his eyes and his mother's heart had been broken and his brother was dead. Swamped in misery, he tripped over a stone and fell full length along the roughness of the road. Scratched and sobbing, he lay, crushed.

Kirsty was no longer screaming, but was slumped on her bed moaning, Mam stroking the top of her arm.

'He's dead, mammy. He's dead.'

Her mother heard but could not respond. She herself was in a state of shock. She had been fond of Murdo, if a bit uncertain about the match between his studiousness and her daughter's exuberance. Kirsty had been so fond of him, though, and she had not tried to interfere. She was distressed by her daughter's anguish and upset by the death of a lad she knew. But what had really stunned her had been the unmistakable swelling of Kirsty's stomach she'd felt through her gown. As she had consoled her daughter she had embraced her as she had done when she was a little girl. The pressing of Kirsty's distended belly against her had not registered immediately, but when it did it stung her as if a wasp had been inside her head. Brusquely she had led her stumbling daughter to her bed and there they now were; one broken-hearted by the final whipping away of all hope, the other aghast. Her daughter was expecting a bastard child.

She felt torn by anger towards Murdo and guilt that she should think badly of the dead. What could they do? How could she have failed to notice, how could she have been so blind? She found herself thinking that perhaps Murdo was better off dead, he at least would not have to face the disapproval of the community and worst of all, of the church. He had died a hero's death and no one would think ill of him. But what was to become of Kirsty? She stared at the pitiful heap that was her daughter and her heart fought a struggle between unconditional pity and unforgiving contempt. How could this have happened? Had she not been raised as a God-fearing girl? Had the warnings rumbling from the pulpit not scared her enough? Had she no respect for herself? She looked at her daughter and she saw, not a grown woman, but her own wee girl, needing her mother now, more than she had ever done.

Annie interrupted her train of thought.

'What's wrong?'

'It's Murdo,' said her mother, her voice fading to a breath. 'He's been killed.'

Kirsty let out a loud groan and turned suddenly to face away from her mother. To hear the horror actually put into words was to have raw spirits thrown onto the fire in her heart.

Annie sat down heavily on the bed beside her mother, her eyes wide.

'What happened?'

'We don't know. Alasdair came to tell us a few minutes ago. His mother must have got the telegram. The poor woman. That's her lost her husband and now her eldest boy. She must be in a terrible state.'

For Annie there was the shock of someone she knew dying so young, more especially following Kirsty's confessions about their love for each other. She leaned back across the bed and rested her face on the wetness of her sister's cheek.

'Oh Kirsty, Kirsty,' she whispered. There could be no consolation, no comforting words. The best she could do would be to cradle her twin, to let her know that she had someone to hold onto.

She did know for how long she lay with her sister. The sobbing subsided, but tears still pulsed slowly from Kirsty's staring eyes. Her breaths were irregular and short, as if they were an afterthought. Annie felt her mother's hand touch her on the shoulder. Her cheek felt like ice as she lifted it from her sister's face. Kirsty did not move, not even her eyes. Her mother was beckoning her out of the room. Annie lifted herself from the bed and pulled a blanket over Kirsty and stroked her head. She moved through to the living room and saw her mother sitting at the table, one hand clenched, the knuckles knocking rapidly and silently on the wood.

'Annie, did you know?' her mother asked sternly.

Annie was taken aback. 'How could I have known? You told me yourself.'

'Not about Murdo, about Kirsty.'

Annie thought for a moment. Kirsty had sworn her to secrecy, but her mother clearly knew.

'You mean about America?'

Mam looked confused. 'America? What about America? I mean Kirsty. I mean Kirsty and the baby she's carrying.'

Annie was stunned and her mother could see it.

'She's carrying a baby,' she explained in a softer tone which immediately hardened as she said, 'And the father of it is now dead.'

Annie tried to take in what had been said. The fire crackled and the clock ticked as they always had, but in a matter of moments life had changed forever. Annie dropped herself into a chair. Her mother went over to the large, blackened kettle that hung permanently over the fire and poured boiling water into the teapot, which she placed on a grid on top of the peat fire. Water sizzled down its side towards the open flame. She returned to her chair at the table.

'What are we going to do?'

'What has Kirsty said?'

'Nothing. She never told me. She doesn't know that I know. I wonder if she even knows herself?'

Another drop of water sizzled on the fire. Mam stared at the floor and sighed deeply through her nose. Annie bit her bottom lip, her eyes darting from the floor, to her mother, to the table. She had seen her mother every day of her life, had seen her every facet through joy and misery. She knew her better than she knew anyone. Now, though, she did not understand her mother's reaction and it made her desperately uncomfortable.

'If I didn't know,' Mam thought aloud, staring now at the fire, 'then nobody else can know. If her own mother couldn't tell, how could anyone else?'

Annie looked at her uncomprehendingly. No one may know

just yet, but they soon would.

'I'm thinking that no one need ever know.'

'How are they not going to know, Mam?'

'If we can get Kirsty away over to town, or maybe even the mainland. She could have the child and come back. No one would know about a baby.'

'But Mam, won't they ask where she is?'

'Yes, yes. Well we tell them that she has gone away because of what's happened to Murdo. Maybe she followed the fishing, or maybe we tell them she's gone south to help with the war. Mairi Isabel is working in a munitions factory in Glasgow. That's what we can say.'

'But Mam, these are awful lies we'd be telling.'

'I know,' Mam snapped. 'What else can we do? She can't have the baby here. She's only a young girl. What's going to happen to her if she's got a baby without a husband? God forgive me, but I don't see what else we can do.'

The minister was already on his way to see Murdo's mother. Word had spread through the village and one of the elders had come to the manse to inform him, catching him unawares. He'd been agitated. His mornings were usually his own, and the whisky he surreptitiously supped late at night when the prayers were done and the flock dispersed could fade away. Another lad dead since he'd sent the boys off to war. This was where he had to prove his worth as a pastor. In the pulpit the serried ranks before him were attendant if not always attentive. He was preaching to the converted. They were in God's house and they were there to hear His Word. Now though he was trudging through the rain to soothe suffering, to try to explain why God had allowed this tragedy. The truth was that he would do so by rote. He himself was struggling to comprehend and to understand; he had been for some time.

He had come to God at his own personal nadir, soaked in alcohol and urine and flailing for something to cling to. God had called to him from the distant teachings of his childhood and he had seized Him with the zeal of the convert. It had saved him literally and, he had believed, spiritually. But now doubt was stalking him, whispering to him in the darkness and unsettling him.

Always in the darkness, always when he felt most alone. As God had been there for him before, so the whisky whispered to him again, 'Just once more, just the one.' And he had tasted its burning kiss once again.

Now he walked through the rain, the elder by his side repeating how terrible it was. How awful that a house that had already lost its father should now lose its eldest boy. Reverend MacIver inclined his head in solemn agreement, the rain soaking his neck, making it rub against his stiff dog collar. He was trying to remember what Murdo looked like. He had a vague picture of a quiet young man with intelligent eyes, but he was not one of those who eagerly grasped his arm after every sermon. He knew his mother though, an honest, genuine, respectful woman, like so many in the congregation. What could he say to her?

There was a stillness around, unusual for a weekday, despite the rain. The church stood on the main road that ran away past the lochside to other parts of the island. Four other roads joined it within yards of each other forming a staggered junction; three leading to other villages and one to the pier. On any day you would expect to see people on the roads. Not today. Only one figure, whom he recognised as one of his elders, was hurrying towards him. That was all. Some of the houses did not even have the smoke from the fires curling from them. It was unsettling.

'Oh minister!' gasped the elder as he reached him. 'You've heard then. What a terrible day it is. Three of our boys are gone.'

'Three?'

The minister was startled.

'Three telegrams today. Three of them have gone.'

'Who? I know of Murdo Morrison. Who else?'

'Murdo Nicolson. And Donald Martin is missing.'

'Oh Lord have mercy on their souls.'

Three of the village's young men swept away. The death of Calum Morrison before had shaken the district, but this was cataclysmic. Almost half of the lads who had proudly strode away barely nine months before were now dead. He had seen them off, grasped their hands and told them that the Lord was with them.

Now they were with Him and would not be returning. Four young lads dead, and for what? The Germans weren't landing on the shore here. They weren't even landing on the shores of the English coast far south. Why had these four lads died?

The minister came back from his doubt and saw his elders looking at him. In the distance he could now see movement stirring throughout the village; news was spreading. These were not names on a list, these were boys whom everyone knew, names and faces that were the future of the community. And now they were gone. No one would be unmoved. And in the homes of the boys who were lost there would be misery unknown before. He must go and minister to their anguish.

Other elders had gathered at the door of Murdo's home, talking with a knot of neighbours. They parted as the minister approached and then followed him, uninvited, into the house. The scene was one of tragic peace. Murdo's mother sat rocking gently on a chair, gazing at the fire in the middle of the floor, holding a young child tightly on her lap. A youth sat drenched and bloodied, his eyes empty. Another, younger boy stood helpless at the dresser. The eldest daughter was preparing food. She did not want to eat, but it kept her busy and there would be visitors.

'Oh, Minister. Hello,' she said gratefully as he came through the door.

Murdo's mother looked startled, absurdly anxious that she had not been at the door to greet him. She made to stand, grasping his hand.

'It's alright, it's alright,' he said kindly, 'You just stay where you are.'

'Children. Children, give the minister a seat.'

The sisters and brothers of the dead man made way for the men of God who had come to bring comfort. They lowered themselves solemnly into the chairs and onto the bench that ran along one wall. The children now stood and watched.

'It's a terrible thing that has happened to you,' Reverend MacIver said presently. 'I take it there is no doubt?'

'No,' said his mother, barely able to say the word.

'It is not for us to know why the Lord has chosen Murdo,' he began softly.

He saw the bereaved mother clinging to his words, her eyes filling with tears, the fingers of her left hand tightly wrapped in her right hand. His was the power to guide her through her grief and it made him feel strong. Through the mumbled prayers and the readings from the Holy Book, he was in command. He, Reverend Calum MacIver, was given unquestioning respect and though he would deny it to himself, it chased the doubt and made him feel good.

Murdo leaned over and kissed Kirsty softly on the cheek. Her hand moved to touch his touch and hold it to her so that he never left her. She gazed at him, but the harder she looked the more indistinct he appeared. She stretched out her other hand to him, straining into the mist for him, but he was walking slowly backwards into the gloom and she felt her fingers scrape against a cold hardness. She strove all the more to reach him, calling to him piteously as he drifted into a blur, his smile beckoning, but with tears in his eyes. She twisted her body to try to rack her arm ever closer to him and then suddenly she felt a sharp chill and the touch of a worn palm on her head.

'Eeesht, my darling, eesht.'

Murdo was gone from sight. Her fingers scrabbled against the stone wall and her calls to him now sounded like nothing more than the whimpers of a wounded dog.

'Mammy is here, my darling, mammy is here,' a voice soothed.

Reality swooshed over her again like a splunge in a wave. Murdo was gone. America was gone. Life stretched ahead into grey nothingness.

She could not bear to think of how Murdo had died. Had he been alone? Had there been pain? Had he thought of her as the last breath slipped away? She could not deal with that now. The emotional agony seemed to bring with it a physical pain. Her lower back ached and her breathing was uncomfortable. She became aware too, that although her body was sweating beneath the blankets of her bed, her groin and her legs were wet, very wet. And her back ached some more.

7

THE ACHE IN HER BACK was soon overtaken by a cramp in her abdomen. It gripped her, contracting her innards, as if some unseen force within was pulling her in on herself. The pain was indescribable. She could barely breathe. She writhed in panic, fearful that she might be dying.

Was it possible to die of sorrow? Was this her heart breaking? Then it passed quickly away.

Her mother, stroking her head, had felt the involuntary tensing. She had heard her daughter's breath catch suddenly and repeatedly. She held her own breath, but said nothing. Surely it could not be so soon? She'd had no time to prepare. What was she to do? She would wait until the next one and that would tell her how long they might have. For the moment she continued caressing her daughter's hair.

Kirsty lay curled beneath the bedclothes. Mam could see only her back, which swelled and fell with her breathing. The love she felt for her daughter was overwhelming. Whatever anger she had, she knew her daughter needed her and she could never abandon her.

Fifteen minutes later Kirsty sucked air through her teeth as once again the pain seized her, seemingly grinding her organs against each other. She let out an involuntary moan of distress and understood that now it was time. The devil was to be released from her womb and she could no longer pretend. The next few hours would take her into the gaping mouth of hell. There would be no escape. She wished she was dying of a broken heart, then at least the living horror would be over. The terrors of damnation were as nothing to knowing that she would never know Murdo again, even beyond this life. She wanted the devil within to burst from her belly and leave her dead. If it did not finish her, then the look of betrayal she would see in her mother's eyes surely would. She must get away. Where, she didn't know, but she must hide, get away from the confines of the house.

Mam felt her try to pull herself out of bed and gripped her hand.

'I've got to get out Mam, I've got to get out,' she said in staccato bursts.

'Kirsty,' she said firmly. 'You are going nowhere. You couldn't go anywhere.'

'I need fresh air, Mam.'

'Kirsty, Kirsty. Stop struggling. Listen to me. I know. I know what's happening to you.'

The contraction passed and Kirsty slumped, looking at her mother.

'Oh Mammy,' she whimpered. 'Oh Mammy, I'm sorry, I'm sorry.'

Her voice fell away and her mother caressed her head and held her close.

'I'm here lass, I'm here.'

'Mammy, I am so sore.'

'I know, my darling, I know. And it will get sorer. It will get sorer and it will get longer and you will just have to be strong. I will be here for you, but I am not going to tell you that it will be easy. Nothing can prepare you for what you are about to go through. Just know this; it is what the woman's body is made for and the Lord will give you the strength to get through it. I did it with you and now you can do it too.'

'What's going to happen to me, Mam? After it's born?'

'I don't know, lass. The first thing to do is make sure that with God's Will, you get through it. Tell me how it happened.'

For the first time a chill came into her mother's voice.

'And how you let it happen?'

'I didn't let it happen, Mammy,' said Kirsty, beginning to sob again.

'Did Murdo force himself on you? I wouldn't have thought....'

'It wasn't Murdo.'

The simple statement, barely audible, jarred Mam.

'It wasn't Murdo?' she repeated.

'It wasn't Murdo,' wept Kirsty. 'And I don't know who it was.'

This was too much for her mother to take in. It wasn't Murdo and she didn't know who it was? Then Kirsty spoke again.

'Somebody forced himself on me. It was the night of the Road Dance.'

Now that she had broken her silence, Kirsty felt more composed. She became more fluent.

'It was the night of the Road Dance. Somebody attacked me when I went away into the moor. He grabbed me, Mam, and he hurt me. He hurt me very badly. I don't even remember much because he banged my head against a rock and I blacked out. I tried to stop him, Mam, but he was holding me from behind.'

'And you don't know who it was?'

'It was dark and he was behind me. His voice was a hiss. It wasn't one that I knew.'

'And was… Did he… Did he?' Mam was hesitant. 'Did he put himself inside you?'

Kirsty's calm slipped. She bowed her head and the tears spilled down again.

'I don't know. I think he must have. I was awfully sore. He banged my head when I was trying to get away and I passed out. When I came round, I was sore… down there.'

There was a long pause.

'I think he must have,' she repeated dejectedly.

Mam sat in silence. How could this be, here of all places? There was an animal amongst them, a beast who had ruined her daughter. What had brought the devil here? Why was God punishing them?

Kirsty began to wince again as another wave of pain smothered her. For the next few minutes, Mam occupied herself with easing her daughter's distress. The pain was as intense as the last time for Kirsty, but she at least felt released from the burden of keeping her predicament a secret. Her mother knew and had not condemned her. While she knew that the pain would intensify, she felt an overwhelming relief that she was not alone.

As the labour pain passed again, Kirsty lowered herself back down and closed her eyes. It gave Mam time to think. That the birth of an illegitimate child would ruin Kirsty's reputation was not in question. Any explanation that Kirsty had been raped might be accepted on the face of it, but the whispers would begin that Kirsty had brought this upon herself; Old Peggy, the twisted old witch would say that Kirsty was trying to save her reputation. And Old Peggy would not keep these thoughts to herself, she would have to share her cynicism with others and the weed of her words would spread.

Mam believed her daughter unreservedly. Why should the girl have her life devastated by an act of evil of which she was the victim? This child was the devil's child. It would bring pain and misery and unhappiness throughout its life. It would always be unloved and unwanted. Its life would be wretched. However she considered it, Mam saw that without the child there would be no dilemma.

'Kirsty, lass, who else knows of this?' she asked quietly.

The Reverend MacIver left Murdo's mother with an assurance that he would return to help her organise a memorial service for her boy, who had made the ultimate sacrifice for his family and for God.

'We bow ourselves before thy infinite Wisdom,' he intoned in a closing prayer, 'And unto Him be the praise.'

There was sniffling and a shuffling of chairs when he finished. He gravely shook the hand of Murdo's mother, clasping both his palms over her knobbly fist. One by one his elders grimly did likewise. The children of the house lined respectfully along the wall, next to the door. The minister swept past them, outside into the rain.

It had been a difficult visit, but the woman had maintained a dignity that he had seen often on the island, a stoicism that he admired. There had been a time when he would have lingered with the grieving, talked to them and listened to them, reassuring them that while he could not know, their loved one had been a Godly person and surely had entered the Kingdom of Heaven.

He found it more difficult now. The fleeting feeling of power he had tingled to when he arrived had been quickly expended. He had sopped too much sorrow, seen too much pain. And worse, he struggled to muster the spiritual fortitude such ordeals required. He admonished himself for leaving Mrs Morrison sooner than he should, but he had nothing more to give. And two other homes needed him, homes like this one where the grief would hang heavy and the future seem bleak and pointless.

Barely had he hunched his shoulders to the rain, when he heard the grieving mother call him. His elders parted as he turned to face her.

'Forgive me Minister, but Murdo was very friendly with young Kirsty MacLeod, Neil MacLeod's daughter. I think they may have had plans. Could I ask that you see she is alright?'

The Reverend MacIver tensed inwardly and nodded his head compassionately.

'Of course. Of course. I'll go there now.'

More grief, more sorrow. And yet, another part of him, the part of him that he wanted to be dominant, marvelled at this poor woman's capacity for compassion in the midst of her own despair. He and his entourage turned to clump solemnly through the downpour.

Annie was taken aback by the sharp rap at the door. Her mother and Kirsty had been alone for some time now. She could hear them speaking, but their voices were muffled and she had not the courage to listen through the door. There had been no shouting or yelling, but there had been suppressed screaming and moaning. She feared for her sister.

The front door had not been closed properly since Alasdair Morrison had arrived to break the news of Murdo's death. Before she could react, the minister put his head round the door. He said 'Hello' as he pushed it open and came into the house, a queue of grey overcoats behind him.

Annie was hesitant and stammering, beckoning the men to be seated with a jumble of incoherent mumblings and gestures. In the moments of their shuffling to settle down, she panicked over what she should do. She did not even know why they were here. Reverend MacIver grew quickly impatient with her uncertainty.

'Is your mother at home?'

'Yes.'

'Do you think I could see her?'

'Yes.'

She did not want to go into the bedroom for fear of what she might see, and yet here was the figure of ultimate authority in the district asking her to do just that.

Her mother entered the room, releasing her from her quandary.

'Oh Minister, I'm sorry, I didn't know you were coming. Annie, you've let the fire go down. Get some peats and get the tea on for the minister.'

'You weren't to know Mrs MacLeod. I've just been to Mary Morrison's.'

'Oh, terrible news, Minister. Murdo was a lovely lad. How is Mary?'

'She's being very strong, very strong indeed. Two other lads in the village have been killed too. It's been a most dreadful day. It's a terrible thing right enough, but we must accept it as God's Will.'

'Two other boys?'

The minister looked to one of his elders.

'Murdo Nicolson and Donald Martin.'

'Oh, my, my! Terrible. Three boys. And Calum Morrison as well. Such good boys.'

'Yes. Yes indeed. Mary Morrison suggested maybe I should call by. She seemed to think that her Murdo and your Kirsty may have had an understanding between them, and that I ought to see Kirsty.'

In the ensuing hiatus, Annie placed some peats from the bucket onto the open fire, darkening the room, the smothered embers throwing out sparks of protest. Smoke spiralled towards the hole in the roof. Mam was uncomfortable.

'An understanding?' she asked.

'Yes. Mrs Morrison seemed to believe that Murdo and Kirsty were close.'

'Well yes, yes, I suppose they were close. He was a nice boy.'

'Is Kirsty alright? Is she at home?'

'Yes, yes she's home. She's a bit upset, but she'll be alright.'

'I thought I would maybe speak to her, perhaps say a prayer for her.'

'That's very kind of you, Minister, but she's actually asleep at the moment and I think maybe that is best for her.'

Mam was horrified. She was lying to the minister. And before he had arrived, she had thought thoughts that she did not think she was capable of. Reverend MacIver was clearly taken aback at this rebuff.

'Well, I can understand that,' he said unconvincingly. 'I'll be at the manse for most of the day if she does want to see me. And I think we should have a service at the church tonight to pray for those poor lads.'

A muffled moan drew everyone's attention to the bedroom door. Another, more intense, quickly followed. The minister looked sharply at Mam.

'Are you sure she's alright?'

There was a pause.

'She must be having a bad dream. Annie, go and see to your sister.'

Annie looked dismayed. She stood motionless, holding a jug of water, about to pour it into the kettle.

'Now!' snapped her mother.

The water spilled as Annie hurried towards the door, conscious of everyone in the room watching her, but she was more concerned with what she might see in the next room.

'Is everything alright?' the minister persisted.

'Yes, yes, yes. Kirsty was upset when she heard.'

Annie had pushed the door with her shoulder, slipped into the room quickly, and pulled it closed again behind her. Her sister was sitting on the edge of their bed, bending forward and moaning. Annie could not see her face clearly, but the skin on her neck and cheeks was vivid red. She dumped the jug on the floor and ran to her sister.

'Kirsty! Kirsty!' she whispered urgently. 'What's wrong? What can I do?'

Kirsty waved her hand and sat up, puffing her cheeks and breathing quickly. A shank of pain stretched through her body forcing her to grimace helplessly. She began to whine in a high pitch tone.

'Oh Kirsty. The minister is here and he can hear you. What can I do?'

Next door, conversation had resumed between Mam and the minister. Kirsty propped herself on her elbows, her chin resting on her breastbone, waiting for the spasm pain to fade and return, as it surely would. The pressure pushing down on her was more than she thought her body could bear.

Mam was showing the minister to the door with scarcely concealed haste. He knew he was being hustled off, and it astounded him. It was normally he who was anxious to break away, who wished he could escape the endless cups of tea and the speaking for speaking's sake. This offended his dignity.

'Your husband is away at the fishing just now, isn't he? And your son?'

It was more of a statement than a question. Reverend MacIver paused and gave Mam a hard look, while the elders walked on outside.

'Yes indeed. Things haven't been so good round this coast, so they are trying the mainland. We're just waiting for their return. I was worried about Neil going to the fishing, but when you hear of those poor boys it makes me thankful he has.'

'Well indeed. We will see you tonight then?'

'Yes, yes. Of course, Minister.'

By now she was speaking to him with her head round the door.

'I'll tell her that you called. And thank you Minister, thank you.'

She thudded the door closed. A few moments later she heard the footsteps tramp away. She ran straight in to see Kirsty.

Reverend MacIver was not going to return to the MacLeod house to be humiliated. His elders had been shocked at the lack of deference. How could anyone behave like that to the minister? Whatever the grief in the house, he, of all people, deserved respect. What troubled the Reverend MacIver even more was that he had been strangely disappointed at not seeing Kirsty. He'd admired her from the pulpit, her weave of red hair vibrant before him in the gloom of greys and browns. His eye had always been drawn to her and he found her pleasing. He would have liked to see in her the devotion and respect that he saw glowing from other women in the congregation. He would never have her physically, but if he could have her adoration that would be compensation enough; he could never be accused of acting wrongly and he could defend himself before God. This visit might have been a way through to her, but he'd been spurned and it rankled.

Mam was with Kirsty by the time the minister and his assembly had reached the road. Her face glistened with perspiration and her teeth were grinding. She had grabbed fistfuls of the bedclothes trying to hold on to something, desperately seeking release. Mam knew the first was usually the worst, the muscles were still young, taut and resistant. The next few hours would be difficult for both Kirsty and the baby, and she could not seek outside help. She would have to be strong for her daughter and draw on her own experience. She believed what she had told Kirsty, that childbirth was a natural process and should hold no fear. But she knew too of women whose body had not been strong enough, women who had some pelvic distortion which made it impossible to give birth, women who had died, weakened by exhaustion and blood loss, while the baby suffocated in its mother's womb as her muscles tried to push it out, but her bones caged it in. Kirsty was a big, strong girl, but that did not guarantee it would all go well. If there were problems she resolved to deal with them when she had to. She could not involve anyone else now.

And so the day dragged on, following a repeating pattern. Outside, the wind rose and the rain fell. At least it kept people in their homes. For that Mam was grateful. Kirsty would be seized by a roll of pain, which would writhe and contort her. Gradually it would subside and she would be left panting and moaning. Mam would urge her to rest, to preserve her strength, waiting for the next surge. And when it came breaking in again she would be there, holding her girl, feeling her tremble and grip so hard that her hand would be left numb and bloodless.

The time between the contractions gradually shortened. Darkness fell early outside and Mam did not know. Time had become nothing but the space between Kirsty's agonised squeals. The wind found its way through the two walls of stone and caused the candles to flicker, projecting ghoulish images on the walls. It was a ghostly scene, with the wailing and the whispering emphasising the air of unreality. There was a chill around the perimeter of the room where fresh air tried to encroach. At the bedside there was suffocating warmth; Kirsty was drenched in sweat, the sheets of the bed crumpled and warmly damp. Mam had removed her outer clothes and still her cheeks burned. Annie moved back and forth through the house, obeying Mam's instructions, bringing whatever was asked for. She was desperate, anxious for her sister, but unable to confront what was going on. She tried to detach herself and hope that time would pass quickly and it would be over and done with.

'You're nearly there, lass, you're nearly there,' Mam encouraged. Kirsty was pushing hard, her face contorted. Resisting the pain, she had decided, was futile. She would have to confront it. There would be a peak that would come sooner or later and she had resolved that she would use her strength to try to hasten it. The suffering would be no less, but it might pass more quickly. The pressure as she pushed was becoming almost unbearable, so she bore down some more.

Her mother was now bending her legs.

'Lift yourself, if you can. Lift yourself. Annie, get in here.'

Annie rushed through the door again, wringing her hands on her apron.

'Hold your sister. Keep pushing girl, but stop when the contraction stops. I can see the head and hair. It can't be long now for you lass, it can't be long.'

Barely had the contraction passed and Kirsty panted for breath, than another one consumed her. She knew herself that there could not be long left as she felt her vagina bulge and not retract when the contraction finished.

Mam was anxiously looking and talking. Kirsty could feel her fingers trying to stretch her. Annie fearfully clasped her sister's hand.

'Come on. You're going to be fine. It's nearly out.'

Kirsty screamed and her face remained agonised after the sound faded to silence.

'It's coming, lass, it's coming.' Mam was breathless now, her face wincing. 'One last time.'

Kirsty felt herself tearing, but there was no extra pain from that. It could not get any worse. She was so tired though, so tired.

'One last time. One last time,' Mam urged.

Kirsty did not feel as if she was part of herself. There was no constructive thought. Her body and muscles seemed to have no use for her mind. She held her breath and spread her hands, as if her body was telling her that every last fragment of strength must be used to push down. With an emphatic heave she felt the block in her birth passage ease as the baby's head emerged into the dim light.

'You're nearly there, girl. That's the worst over.' Mam sounded almost elated now.

The baby's shoulders and torso slipped out quickly as Mam pulled its head. Kirsty was conscious of her body expelling with a surge what had tormented her for so long.

'It's a boy,' Mam said matter-of-factly as she placed the child on the bed. Kirsty felt the heat of him next to her and the stretch of the umbilical cord across her leg. She pulled away from her son and felt a sudden draught where he had lain next to her. Mam vigorously tied cotton knots round the cord.

'Annie, get me a knife.'

Kirsty felt her sister drop her hand and for the first time in several hours there was no direct human contact, other than the tenuous link of the lifeline between her and her baby. The constant overwhelming cramp was receding, although there was a sharper, more irritating smarting where her skin had torn.

'It's not over yet, lass, though the worst is passed,' Mam said as she briskly hacked at the umbilical cord. 'The afterbirth will come shortly.' And it did, her birth muscles contracting one more time to push it from her onto the floor.

She collapsed back on the bed and sighed deeply. There was no feeling of relief though. Not the slightest elation. Her ordeal was not over. In some respects it was just beginning.

Mam wiped at her grandson's nose and he suddenly let out a trembling cry that startled his mother. There had been hours of exclamations, of snapped instructions and encouragements.

This was new and alarming. The shrill cry would resound down through the rest of her life. She knew that as she heard it.

Mam picked up the baby and told Annie to spread a towel on the bed. It was the first proper view Kirsty had had of her son. She saw his slicked, light hair, his jerking limbs and the deep purple of his fingernails bold against the stark paleness of his skin. It was a brief glimpse, as Mam placed him down again, and although she could see his hair, she wanted to see all of him again. She wanted to hold him now, to draw him to her and gaze at him. This was not how she had expected it to be. She had wanted to despise the child. But he looked so helpless, so distressed and fragile that she wanted to embrace him.

She waited for Mam to wrap her baby, hoping that she would then give him to her, but not wanting to ask. His crying had diminished, but he still whimpered from within his cocoon of towels. Kirsty felt her breasts swollen and sore. Maybe she should feed him, but Mam seemed to know what to do, so she waited.

'Annie, get me a bucket and then help your sister clean herself up.'

She returned quickly and Mam gathered the placenta from the floor and slopped it into the bucket. 'We'll need to get rid of this. Annie, put it on the fire. Make sure it all burns. There must be no trace left.' Kirsty glanced at her sister and saw her flushed face pale slightly.

'Mam, maybe I should try to feed him,' Kirsty said.

'I don't think that's a good idea,' Mam snapped.

'Why not? He's hungry.'

'You feed him, girl, and he'll know you as his mother. Even worse, you'll feel he's your son, and that'll lead to worse pain. I've got some milk from the cow. I'll give him that.'

'But Mam, I want to help him. My chest is sore and I want to feed him.'

Her mother stared hard at her.

'Understand this, girl. It's better that you have nothing to do with him. Then, when he goes it'll not be so bad for you. Or for him.'

'Then when he goes'. The blunt words jarred Kirsty. She was

being told bluntly that her baby must go. She could hear him sucking hard. She couldn't see his head, but she saw his arm bent towards his mouth. He was sucking on his knuckles.

'Where will he go?'

'I don't know. We'll need to take him over to town and find out where he can go.'

'But Mam, I don't want him to go. He's my baby.'

'He's not your baby. You were made to have him. Where will it leave your life, Kirsty? Who's going to want you? You walk out of this house with that child and people will think you nothing but a common whore.'

Kirsty was crushed by her mother's tone.

'But it wasn't my fault.'

'You think Old Peggy will believe that? They'll say if it wasn't your fault, why did nobody ever know you were expecting a child? What were you hiding? That's what they'll ask. No, girl, if you claim that child as your own, your life is as good as over. No man, maybe no home. What would you do? And your father? What will he say? It's better for you and better for the child that he goes. There are places where he could be looked after and have a better life than he ever could here. Everyone here would know him as the bastard child.'

Never once did Mam look down at her grandson. As she spoke above him, his clenched fist would slip from his mouth and he would move his head from side to side until his open mouth found it again. Then Kirsty would hear the gentle squeak as he sucked hard.

Annie had come back with a bowl of warm water and some cloths and began to wash Kirsty down. Kirsty lay back. She felt so tired. Mam picked up the baby and carried him from the room. Kirsty watched with a growing helplessness.

'Mam. I want to see him again.'

Then she began to sob quietly.

Mam was right. The baby had to go. Anytime she had considered her future after her pregnancy, a child was never there. But now that he was here, she so wanted to keep him, to nurse him. How could something so innocent and perfect be the work of the devil?

'I want to keep him, Mam,' she repeated softly.

Annie had finished wiping her and was pulling the bedclothes over her.

'Don't think of it now. Just rest.'

'Promise me I'll see him again.'

'Just rest, Kirsty.'

With that she walked quickly from the room. Kirsty knew her sister was crying.

Kirsty's baby slept for the first few hours of his life. Mam had fed him with warm milk fresh from the cow. It had been difficult, but she used a teaspoon for him to sook from. She knew that would give him bad wind, but it was better this way. And he winded well, soft burps and mouthfuls of milk slipping out of his mouth when she put him to her shoulder and clapped his back. She felt the warmth of him against her as she rubbed gently between his shoulder blades. How little time ago it seemed since she had done this to her own children. Now she was doing it to her grandchild. And she stopped herself there. He could never be her grandchild.

Annie cleared a pit in the fire. She stood back with the placenta in the bucket, uncomfortable with what she had to do.

'Go on, lass,' Mam beckoned to the fire. 'There can be no sign left.'

Annie knelt down and removed the kettle from its chain above the fire. Then she tipped the bucket slowly with both hands, its contents slithering with a damp thud onto the flames. Almost immediately there was a sizzling and burbling as the fire flared angrily and the placenta blistered and burned. In her bed Kirsty started and the pain bit at her again.

'Go and check on your sister. I'll watch the child,' Mam said. 'That should be gone before the night's out.'

'How is he?' Annie asked.

'He's taken some milk and given me some wind, so he's settled.'

'Does he really have to go, Mam? He's so lovely.'

'What else can we do?' Mam snapped. 'This morning I was thinking about your father and brother at sea in this weather, and tonight I'm holding a grandchild that I never knew was coming. I don't know what to do. But I tell you this, if people find out there's a baby in this house what'll they think of your sister?'

'What does it matter what other people think, Mam?'

'Aye, it might sound fine to say that and people will be kind to your face. Many of them will mean it. But you think of Mary Horseshoe. Remember what happened to her daughter? Oh yes, people might be nice to you, but what are they saying among themselves? What decent man would ever want your sister? And the boy himself. He was born out of sin and he'll never be allowed to forget it. That's no life. Best for him and for Kirsty if we take him over to town and find somewhere new for him.'

Annie just sat gazing at the baby.

'Do you really think I want him to go?' Mam said more softly. 'I'm holding him here and I'm feeling him breathe against me and my heart loves him already. But we've got to think about the future. We've got to think of what's best for him, not us.'

There was nothing more to say. The two women sat in the glow of the fire, Mam rocking gently back and forth, the baby resting in the crook of her arm. And despite herself, Mam gazed upon him, and wondered.

Kirsty never slept. She had lain and endured torture in her mind, worse even than the physical discomfort in the hours after the birth. Unable to rest, she had thought constantly of her baby, straining to hear any sound he might make. She feared that Mam had already taken him away, but then his faint cry would reassure her. Her baby may still be in the house, but for how long? She so wanted to go through to him, to cradle him and tell him she loved him and he would always be hers.

There was movement in the next room. Her mother and Annie were with her son and she felt trapped in her bed. She loathed herself, hated her weakness. But for all that she wanted to burst through and take him to her, she knew she would not. Mam was set that there was no place for him here and while she cared no more for her own reputation, she could see that for her boy to be given the best chance, he must go. But go where? And go to whom? Who would call her baby their son? Who would he grow up to know as his mother? Who would caress his hair as his eyes gazed at them through drooping lids? Who would sing him the songs and tell him the stories of old? And whose image would he carry in his heart until he died as the one he knew as mother? She whipped her head round, face down on the pillow, and sobbed sorely.

As the hours passed and the room cooled to cold, her eyes became dry and sore and her thoughts darkened into the night. Why think he would be taken to another woman who would become his mother? Was there not a home for orphans in the town? A cold dark building, she had recalled hearing before, where there were too many children vying for too little love. Was that to be the destiny of her son: to be cast away unloved, when she had so much love she could give him? There were no tears left to cry, but every time she thought she had reached the depths of her misery, she would slip a little lower. Regardless of how he was conceived, he was her child and she had to do right by him. Nothing could be more dreadful for him than to be abandoned to a loveless life. Nothing. She couldn't let it happen. She had brought him to this world and she must protect him from it, if it was the only thing she did as his mother.

She moved her right leg first, slowly, deliberately. A sharp pain stabbed her when she lifted herself onto her elbow. She was so sore, but she was more determined. Gradually her left leg burrowed out from under the covers until she felt the cold air wrap around it. Now she was twisted in a semi-seated posture on the edge of the bed. She closed her eyes, blew out her cheeks, and pushed herself upright. Her body shivered and trembled, but now she was properly seated. The hardest movement would be standing. She placed her hand against the corner of the stone wall, picking her fingers into any crevice and gripped tightly. She held her breath and heaved herself to her feet, a tortuous spasm tearing the breath from her and causing her knees to buckle. Her grasp on the stone held her steady. She knew she was bleeding, she could feel it ooze down her thigh despite the padding Annie had put on her, but she convinced herself the worst was over.

Annie was sound asleep on their brother's bed. She was still clothed, so she must have been too tired to undress. Kirsty assumed her sister had been watching over her and she loved her for it, but she could not allow herself to waken her.

She shuffled quietly towards the door, wincing with each step. Annie had left the door slightly ajar and Kirsty manoeuvred herself round it. The stiffness was going from her limbs, but she was still sore.

In the living room she saw that the fire had fallen to glowing embers. Mam lay asleep on her chair, her head back and her mouth open, snoring slightly. At her feet, closer to the fire, was the metal bathtub. Arranged within it were two pillows held together by a sheet folded around them. Lying on top of the pillows, underneath the sheet and wrapped in a towel was her baby. Only his face, the front of his head and his left hand could be seen. She was engulfed by love for him. He was sleeping deeply and would remain so until hunger woke him.

A sob caught in her throat. The scene was one of peace and tenderness. Mam watching over him. It would have been fine for it always to be so, but she knew it never could, and it tore at her.

She moved over to the front door, jerked her coat off its peg and pulled it on. Her shoes lay at the door, but she would put them on last. She buttoned up and, hearing the rain pattering on the outside door, flicked the collar up behind her neck. Her movements were easier now. She still felt as if her womb had been pulled from within her, but she was so focused on what she must do, that her mind seemed to blot out the pain.

She padded over to the tub. Mam's head tipped a little and for a moment Kirsty thought she would waken. Her snoring stopped, but she remained asleep. Kirsty knelt beside the tub and worked her hands round underneath the bundle of baby, blanket and pillows. She knew that the slightest movement of the tub would cause it to grate on the clay floor. With one hand supporting the top of the bundle and the other the feet, she lifted it out of the tub. Her baby's face was now just beneath her own and she could really look at him for the first time. From the fading light of the fire, she could see that his hair was sparse, but light coloured.

She fancied that there might be an auburn hue, but that could be a trick of the light. She saw the full lips and the fine nose and she knew that he was her son. She loved him so, and wanted to place her lips on his brow and breathe his smell and hold him to her forever.

He was so well padded that he felt no movement and didn't stir. She carried him silently to the door and pressed her feet into her shoes. Stout leather shoes they were, and she was anxious that their clumping might waken Mam. The big test would be the door. She knew how to open it without scraping the floor; you held the handle and took the weight of it in your shoulder and only let it down when the door had opened. This time she had a baby in one hand and it would not be easy.

She paused, waiting for the right moment. The wind was coming through into the lobby and as soon as she opened the door from the living quarters whirls of wind would rush in. She couldn't delay long. Any moment the baby might cry, or Mam waken to check on him. Shifting the baby to her left arm, she gripped the loose handle in her right hand, took its weight on her shoulder and waited. The wind whooshed outside and the rain pattered in a way that in different circumstances would have exaggerated the warmth and comfort of her home. She was about to leave that security.

The clock ticked slowly. Then she sensed the wind was taking a breath. In two quick movements she swung open the door and span into the lobby and lifted the door closed again behind her. When she opened the front door the storm tried to rush inside, but in an instant she pulled it behind her. She didn't wait to hear whether Mam was awake. She hunched herself over the baby's face and ran quickly up the path, then turned right, on the road towards the shore. The rain drove hard against her face and the wind dragged at her coat. Running was difficult with both arms wrapped round the baby and the pain of the motion was almost crippling. Her shoulders twisted from side to side, barely in rhythm with her stumbling steps. She feared she might fall, but she had to get away from the light cast from the window of the house.

Despite her efforts the rain smacked onto the face of the baby.

He screwed his face tight until his eyelashes were lost beneath the folds of crumpled skin. His tiny, wrinkled hand worked against his face, rubbing at the side of his nose, shocked by the sudden, cold sting. She pulled the towel closer round his head, but still the stabs of rain got through. His tiny mouth opened and let out a weak cry which was whipped away by the wind.

'My darling,' she whispered breathlessly, hugging him closer to her.

Already the water was seeping through her coat onto her shoulders and dribbling down the back of her neck. The stones on the road rasped beneath her soles and then the lip of her shoe caught the tip of a sharp rock poking through the track and she lurched forward, her feet scrabbling to regain her balance.

She had to walk. She looked over her shoulder and could open her eyes properly because the rain was not hitting her face on. There was no sign of activity at the house, no one was following her. It would not be long, though, and she must keep going.

As her initial panic faded, she checked on the baby. He was still crying and she felt for him. Pushed from the warmth of the womb, pulled away from his mother and now being pummelled by a Hebridean storm.

Although the early hours of the morning, it was not dark, it never was at this time of year. In the grey light she could see the deeper shadow of the land against the sky where it rose up around the edge of the sea inlet. In a way, it was better that there was wind and rain. On a better morning, someone might have been out and about.

As she gathered her breath and the adrenalin rush passed, she felt sore again, aching raw and bleeding. But she had to be strong and force herself on. Now she was past the last of the houses. The Skipper would be asleep inside, he had slept through worse storms than this. His house was the first in the village to feel the full blast of the sea. The roar of the Atlantic making landfall was at once wonderful and terrifying. It was as if it was letting loose its rage on the island for breaking its rhythm, as the broken mass of ocean crashed torn and ragged onto the rocky shore. The spray ricocheted onwards, mingling with the rain.

The road petered out, gradually overcome by grass as began its final descent to the sea. As her feet pressed the grass onto the wet stones, she had to be careful of slipping. Her steps were cautious and the smaller, tenser movements of her thigh muscles seemed to free the pain to surge again. She had to stop to catch her breath. The baby cried, his gums angry and red, and his little tongue vibrating with the sound. She released one of the buttons on her coat and slipped the bundle inside. It offered only a little more protection, but she was his mother and she would do as best she could.

The grass reached her knees and the bottom of her nightgown was soaked. As well as the rain, the drops that clung to the grass in the wind ran into her shoe and her feet swelled and the knuckles on her toes rubbed raw against the leather.

Just beyond the wall of The Skipper's croft a rough track meandered up the cliffs, disappearing at clusters of rocks and re-emerging on the other side. This was a sheep track, but it did just as well for the crofters wanting to reach the pastures beyond the village bounds. Kirsty turned onto it just where the road finally surrendered to the mud and grass on the edge of the pebble shore. The rain now slapped the side of her head, rather than coming straight on. The baby was completely sheltered now, but still he cried, a quivering squawk that she could not soothe.

The climb was hard and she throbbed sore, sometimes having to lean her hand on her knee to force herself up. She had clambered here often in her life, but never as now. Her breath came in ever-deepening gulps. But she was past the steepest of the incline. Two hundred feet below the sea boiled and thrashed, and the wind howled by her ears without rest. It tried to force her back and sometimes made her take only a half step. Determined, she pushed on.

The inlet cut about a quarter of a mile into the land. That distance on the road would easily be covered in five minutes. But here on the cliffs, battling with the wind, and minding the grass and the rocks and the jagged indents where a weaker part of the cliff had long given up the struggle, it took her closer to half an hour to reach the point where before her there was no more land, just the open expanse of sea. Here she stopped. This was her journey's end, here at the end of the land on the edge of the world.

The baby was distressed. She clasped her hand to his head, sheltered beneath her coat and leaned forward to kiss him. Then she sat on a slab of rock and gently turned him towards her breast and guided his pained little mouth to the comfort of her nipple. It took a little time, but when he tasted the warmth of his mother's colostrum, the newborn baby sucked greedily and snuffled contentedly, while around him the world raged and his mother, rocking gently back and forth, wept.

When he had had his fill, she kissed him again and nuzzled him. His eyes opened, vivid in the grey of the morning. Then they closed again as nestled against the warmth of his mother.

She would wait until he was asleep. Her mind was feverish and her breath was coming in rapid pants. She muttered prayers that she had absorbed through all the sermons she had been to in her life. They were said for her baby, not for herself. This act would put her beyond redemption and she knew that. But she must plead for her baby.

His movement against her was now still and she thought he must be asleep. The wind was tearing at her, ripping her hair and she was having to force herself against it to keep herself upright. It would calm momentarily and swirl in from behind her, then blast again from the seaward side. It was as if the turmoil in her mind was being paralleled by the natural forces around her.

There was no clear thought in her mind, but using one hand for leverage against the rock, she edged on her knees towards the very edge of the cliff. Her other arm held her baby tight. She couldn't look down. Using her free hand she unbuttoned her coat, which instantly flapped wildly behind her. The baby remained asleep despite being so exposed, the towel and blanket and his mother's arms protecting him from the gale. The only human sound, that of Kirsty's whimpering, was lost in the wind. Her thighs and stomach strained to stop her being blown back. Somewhere deep within her there was a glimmer of relief that maybe she would be unable to do it after all. But the fears that had driven her to this point were still dominant.

She tucked the towel more tightly around the tiny sleeping form, kissed him and whispered, 'I'm sorry, my darling baby.' Then she stretched out her arms, holding him in her hands, her fingers gripping onto the back of the blanket that covered the towel and her head falling onto her chest. Once, twice she released her grip, but instantly dug her fingers back into the blanket again. As her hands went through these spasms her breath ever so slightly steadied.

In an instant the wind from the ocean dropped and swirled and she felt the light weight gone from her arms. Her heart dropped and she cried 'Oh My Lord!' She looked down, her eyes wide, and saw the little bundle fall into the grasping waves below.

8

THE SKIPPER LIKED TO WANDER the shore, especially after a storm. And last night's had been fierce. There was never any telling what treasures it might yield. Wood was common, tree trunks that had fallen into the rivers of North America and by current, tide and wind had crossed the Atlantic. And on an island with no forests because of the acidic peat and strong winds, wood was always useful. Many a Hebridean roof beam had grown on the banks of the St Lawrence. So precious was that wood that in the evictions of dim childhood memory, he remembered people dragging their wood behind them before their houses were put to the torch. They would be the roof beams for the new homes of the displaced. The very dresser in his house had been fashioned from wood he'd gathered over the years.

Bottles were common too, thrown overboard from the fishing boats that followed the herring. Occasionally the writing on what remained of a label told of a ship from a foreign port. He added some of them to the horde of souvenirs he had from his own days at sea. He still remembered sombrely the bottle with the note inside. It had been before education had been compulsory and the only person he could think of who might be able to read it was the minister. He had had scanned it carefully. 'God rest their souls,' he'd sighed. Then he and The Skipper had prayed.

Boxes and barrels, rusty cans and fishing buoys, lengths of rope and lobster creels. And seaweed scattered everywhere. For a time seaweed had been the living for families who gathered it and burned it down for kelp. Of course, soon enough the landlords cast their eyes elsewhere and the lives of the people were disrupted once again. The landlords and their greed and the uncertainty it caused were what had driven The Skipper to the sea. No man could claim to own the high seas.

After a big storm, The Skipper would find fish of all sorts scattered among the rocks and stones, flapping for life in the pools. There had even been whales here. That hadn't been the storms of course. No, the whales sometimes just swam right up into the shallows and let themselves be cast on the shore. There was no reason to it that anyone knew, but they cared little. A whale could provide food, clothing and oil. It didn't go to waste. It had made him laugh when they came in. He'd been at the whaling for a time, down in the South Atlantic. It had been a tough endurance and here they were throwing themselves within yards of his home.

'All the way to South Georgia, and the creatures are arriving on my doorstep,' he would laugh. It was a story he told often in the bothies or at the ceilidhs.

He was of indeterminate age, The Skipper. He had been born at the seeding time when the kelping was good. That was as much as he knew. Folk reckoned that made him about a hundred years old. As long as he had his sight and could walk, he wasn't caring. There wasn't much left of his hearing, though he could hear well enough when he chose. With his dark woollen crew-neck jumper, peaked captain's hat, long white whiskers and pipe, he was a familiar and much-loved character.

He had heard the winds rising last night and knew it would be rough. He'd even gone out to watch the waves before darkness fell. He would be up early to browse on the shore. Until then, as he had done so often at sea, he would pull up the covers and sleep. And so he did.

By mid-morning the winds had blown away and the sea had calmed, as if seeking peace, sore from the night before. The Skipper had himself some porridge before making his way down to the shoreline, only a hundred yards from his home. Stranded jellyfish glistened in the sunshine. There was the fresh salty smell that came before the decay. Yellowing froth quivered beyond the shoreline on the green of the crofts, thrown there by the farthest reaching waves.

The Skipper walked slowly, every now and then balancing on a rock and casting his glance about him like a net. Flotsam was strewn across the beach, but much of it had been broken by the storm. It would take him time to choose what he could use and carry it beyond the tide mark. Every now and again he would sit down, cut some tobacco to pack into his pipe, and watch the sea. Gradually he worked his way around the shallow horseshoe of the bay until the tide was almost fully back in.

He would never know what it was about it that caught his eye. Until he died he would say that sometimes he wished it never had. Maybe the white of it was whiter than the bed of foam in which it floated. More likely, he felt, the fates had decreed that he would find it. Whatever it was, once he'd seen it, he couldn't take his eyes off it.

It floated among the rocks and boulders on the north side of the bay, near to where the most recent cliff fall had been. He kept his eye fixed on it as he moved nimbly from stone to stone, instinctively knowing which would take his weight without rocking. It didn't bob in the movement of the water the way that the foam did. He began to think it might be a seal pup.

It took ten minutes to clamber as close as he could before the cliff rose sheer from the sea and barred his progress any further. In his younger days, he would have thought nothing of swimming out to it, but that was beyond him now. So he waited for the tide to bring its mystery to him, as it surely would. It rose and fell with the motion of the water, some twenty feet away, but he could still not make out what it was. Every swell brought it a little closer, then took it away, not as far, then pushed it towards him again.

He could see now that it was no seal pup, but a cloth bundle. It looked like towels. Eventually, kneeling against a rock, he stretched his arm into the water and tickled it towards him with his fingers. Then with a final push from the sea, he grabbed it and heaved it onto the rocks. Water poured from it like a sponge being squeezed. It wasn't just cloth, there was something inside. Tossing it gently onto another rock, he pulled himself up beside it.

The Skipper had seen a lot in his time at sea. He had pulled drowned men from the water, grotesquely bloated. He'd once hauled a body in with his nets, or rather what was left of it, after the creatures of the deep had had their fill. A gruesome sight it had been, all the more shocking for being so unexpected.

This was worse. He flicked back the edge of a towel and the swollen face of a baby screamed silently back at him, forcing him to recoil in horror, scrabbling back along the rock. He thought his time had come, his heart was exploding in his chest. Bile burned his throat and he coughed it clear.

He hadn't been mistaken. It was a baby for sure. He crawled back towards it. He guessed it hadn't been in the sea too long. A string of seaweed hung from it like a grotesque strand of hair. Otherwise, it was remarkably unmarked. Bloated by the water, yes, but the crabs and the fish had not had a chance to tear at it.

The Skipper was not a man for emotion. He'd never been in love, never felt its glow. His mother had died when he was young, so even maternal affection had never cuddled him close. His father had been a good man, but not a warm one. There had been plenty of women in ports of call, but that was always quick and transient. As soon as he left their bed, they left his life. Maybe had he been at home he might have married, but he never thought it fair to leave a girl for so long. Not that he was ever really at home long enough. There had been opportunities, but they had always seemed to be more of a business transaction than a marriage: typically a widow looking for a provider for her children. And then his life at sea had passed and he had stayed on the land, living in the family home with his sister. When she had died ten years ago he had been on his own and now that's the way he liked it. Once upon a time he might have reflected on what he had missed, no wife, no children, but now he accepted that was how it was.

The sight of the little baby, lying dead before him stirred an unfamiliar tenderness. What had brought it to this terrible end? Like him, the child had been separated from its mother, even in death. Had she held her babe until she could hold him no more? Had he cried as he slipped from her grasp and she drifted away on the ocean? He lifted the pathetic, sodden bundle and carried it to his home.

'In God's name, Kirsty, what have you done?' Annie screamed at her through the wind. Kirsty didn't respond. Annie grabbed her shoulders and pulled her round to look at her, but Kirsty seemed to be in a trance. Her hair was smeared across her face and her eyes were dull.

A blur of panic had brought Annie here. The yell of her mother that the baby had gone and Kirsty was gone too. She must find them. Find them and bring them back. She must go now, now before anyone saw them. And as Mam yelled and ran through the house, Annie pulled on her boots and coat and headscarf and stepped out into the wind and the rain. With the rain behind her, she could see some distance ahead. There was no sight of Kirsty.

She stopped to think. Kirsty had kept her pregnancy a secret, she didn't want anyone to know. It was unlikely then that she would have run through the village, with the chance of being spotted or stopped. She would have stayed away from the road. To avoid clambering over dykes and walking down crofts, she would have had to go towards the shore, climb up the hills and work her way back along the perimeter of the village through the moor. Annie turned and ran back down towards the shore. As she passed the house, Mam was at the door of their house, distractedly working her hands on her pinny.

'Have you seen them? Her coat and shoes are gone. What is she doing?'

The last unanswerable question was lost to Annie as she kept on towards The Skipper's house. From there she could skirt round the back of the crofts and hopefully catch her. Kirsty would be in no condition to move quickly or far. Annie couldn't be angry with her sister. What must she be feeling even to think of running away?

As she reached the track to the grazings, she saw fresh scrapings in the earth where someone, and it could only be Kirsty, had slipped and slithered on her way up the trail. Annie thought of her sister, fleeing desperately with her baby and she had to quell the tears. Her sister was fleeing like a frightened animal, and she was the hunter.

Annie scrambled up the track. She would bring Kirsty home and promise her that her baby would be remaining with her. What primal instinct was driving her on through her suffering to protect her baby? Where was she going, where could she go, how long since she'd gone?

At the top of the hill Annie followed the track as it wound off into the hinterland of peat banks and rocky outcrops, losing itself in bogs and lochans. There was no sign of her sister. How far could she have gone with her strength drained and her body torn? Annie stopped and looked around seeing nothing but the sweeps of rain.

'Kirsty! Kirsty!' she shouted, but the wind thrust her calls back at her.

She ran on further, but still saw nothing, not a movement nor a footprint. Her own feet were sinking into the peat, but she could see no other traces of the earth having been disturbed by feet. She started to retrace her steps to the top of the trail. Where else could Kirsty have gone? A scuff of fresh earth and grass stuck to a rock drew her eyes and Annie realised that Kirsty had not doubled back along the village perimeter. She was heading to the cliffs. Annie had felt shock, panic and sympathy, now she felt fear. Her throat contracted and her mouth dried and she ran as fast as she dared along the cliff edge.

Then she saw Kirsty sitting as if staring at the sea and she slowed to a relieved walk. She did not want to scare her by running to her because the wind was blowing directly past Kirsty and she would hear nothing behind her. As she walked the fifty yards towards her sister, Annie tried to catch her breath in the wind. She wanted to hold her and tell her it would alright, that they could stare down convention and the baby need never leave them. But as she came close she could see no sign of the baby. There was the roar of the sea and the stinging spray and Kirsty's drained and vacant face. The horror punched her hard.

'In God's name, what have you done? You can't have, Kirsty. You can't have.'

Kirsty didn't move, didn't look, wasn't hearing. Annie grabbed her shoulders.

'Kirsty, where is the baby?'

There was no response.

Annie trembled and screamed, but the wind whipped the sound

from her mouth and sent it tumbling into the empty expanse of the moor. She scrambled to the precipice and looked over in the vain hope that she might see something, anything that might save them from this nightmare. But the sheer power of the waves pounded any lingering hope.

Annie tried to steady herself. She had to get Kirsty home. She hauled her sister to her feet, expecting her to be a dead weight, but Kirsty offered no resistance and seemed willing to be led. Annie slipped her right arm around her and rested Kirsty's head on her shoulder. Then they walked away from the roaring ocean, the craggy cliffs and the scene of Kirsty's awful deed. But the deed itself lay heavy upon them and they would never leave it behind.

It was still gloomy, but some people would be up already, checking their beasts or gathering eggs from the hens for breakfast.

They reached the road by The Skipper's house and Mam was waiting. She had been unable to stay in the house, but could not let herself stray too far in case Kirsty returned. The wind was abating, but the rain still fell heavily. Mam ran to them.

'Where were they?'

'Wait till we get into the house Mam.'

'Are you alright, girl?'

'Wait till we get to the house Mam,' Annie insisted.

Mam took Kirsty's free arm and pulled it round her shoulders, but it was more a hindrance than a help.

'I've got her, Mam. You just go on ahead.'

'How can I? What's happened? What's the matter?'

'For God's sake do as I'm telling you,' hissed Annie.

Mam flinched, but did as she'd been told.

At last they reached the temporary sanctuary of the house. Mam slammed the door behind them. She took control again.

'Get that child out of that coat. Let's get her in front of the fire. What possessed her?'

'Mam,' Annie interrupted, 'the baby isn't there.'

'Where is he then?'

'Mam.'

Annie's tone made Mam stop.

'Mam. I think the baby is gone.' Annie spoke deliberately.

'Gone?'

'I think Kirsty has got rid of the baby.'

Mam's eyes were uncomprehending.

'I think she's thrown him off the cliff.'

There was a startling wail from Kirsty who suddenly came alive, throwing herself onto the floor, her fingers clawing out and her toes working against it as if she were trying to climb away from some terrible threat.

Mam flung her arms around her and spoke loudly, trying to calm her.

'Kirsty, lass, Kirsty. You're safe. We're here with you.'

Kirsty twisted herself around and stared at her mother.

'I've killed him, Mam. I've killed my baby.'

The police house was a modern, stone-built, whitewashed cottage with a slate roof. Built near the church, the school and the crossroads, it was at the heart of the district. It doubled as police station and home for John MacRae, his wife and young daughters.

In years to come, he would remember much of the detail of this day, but not how it began. It would have been much like any other until the door rapped and Mary, his wife, answered it. He could smell the freshness of the rain from his desk where he was going through the mail Peter the Post had brought shortly before. John could hear the tones of a man's voice before his study door swung open. It was The Skipper, the familiar carved face and long white beard damp beneath a waxed wide-brimmed fisherman's hat. His stooped frame wrapped in a cape of the same material.

'Skipper!'

'Constable.'

The Skipper's use of the official term made it clear that this was no courtesy call.

'I hope you haven't walked all this way in this rain?' asked the policeman, knowing that the question needed no answer. 'It's terrible out there. Take your cape off and have a seat.'

'Ah well Constable, I think maybe I'm as well to keep it on and maybe you'll need to get your own on. There's something you should see.'

'Oh?'

'Aye,' The Skipper sighed, 'and I'm afraid it's not a good sight.'

'Oh?' The tone of the policeman was already graver.

'I have the body of a wee baby in my house. I found him floating in at the shore.'

MacRae stared at him.

'I don't think he'd been in the water long.'

The policeman rubbed his forefinger along his upper lip, thinking.

'My, my. A body? A baby you say? Was there any sign of anyone else? Nobody else in the water?'

The Skipper shook his head.

'Did you see any boats?'

'I did not. And to be truthful, John, I think it would have to have been very close to the shore in the first place for the child to be washed up so soon, untouched.'

Constable MacRae was pulling his cape over his head.

'Did you see anything else unusual?'

'No I did not.'

'Well I better go and see it.'

In the walk through the village, the policeman got the old man to tell him the story in full detail. The rain was now a light smirr and some of the villagers had come outside. They saw the tall, long-striding policeman, and the stooped, bearded figure of The Skipper. They threw greetings, loaded with the unasked question of what was going on. They were acknowledged brusquely and the two men carried on, leaving a widening wake of wonder.

The policeman's pace made no allowance for the other man's age and The Skipper would not have expected it. Before they had reached the house the men had lapsed into silence. The Skipper had told John MacRae everything. There was nothing more could be said and no other subject worthy of discussion. As they rounded the final bend, the shore came into view. With the wind dropping, the sea was not thrashing as it had been before, although there was still a noticeable swell. A heavy sea mist hung like a drab curtain at the end of the bay, hiding the ocean from sight.

The Skipper pushed open his door and led the way in, neither man waiting to shake the rain off. The smell of peat smoke and fish was strong in the house. Smoke still curled from the whitened clumps of peat. As MacRae accustomed his eyesight to the gloom, the older man simply pointed to his box bed.

'The wee soul's in there. I couldn't think of what else to do with him.'

The policeman could make out a grey shape in the dimness. It seemed so small, so insignificant, but the policeman sensed that its impact would shake this community to its very core.

As he moved towards through the shroud of smoke and murk, it seemed almost to fluoresce. MacRae leant over the bundle, bracing himself for what he might see and saw that the old man had tried to bestow some sort of dignity by covering the face. As The Skipper had done before him, he gently, oh so gently lifted the towel, still damp and heavy, as if fearful that he may stir the infant child from slumber.

There was no recoil. The baby seemed to be asleep, that was all, here in the shadows of the old man's house.

'I didn't want to leave him alone,' The Skipper was explaining sadly. 'I didn't want to leave him, but I couldn't carry him through the village. I thought that maybe here might be best.'

The policeman had children of his own, had watched them fall asleep so often, and this poor baby could have been one of them, save for a slight puffiness around his face. And the cold; he was so, so cold. Such were the fine distinctions between the living and the dead. Constable MacRae looked at the child, innocent and lost, and felt the tears in his eyes.

'You know it's a boy?' he asked almost too gruffly, official action suppressing the human reaction.

There was a pause.

'Well I don't, right enough. I just took it to be that he was. I'm sorry.'

'There's nothing you need be sorry for,' the policeman said as he slowly unravelled the towels. 'You've done as best for the wee soul as anyone could.'

The pathetic sight of the baby's body, and especially its

clenched fists, fired an anger through him. The ragged stump of the umbilical cord with the tightly knotted cotton tourniquet still in place forced him to consider, not as a worst-case possibility, but as the terrible likelihood, that this had not been any sort of accident. The brutal reality must be that the infant had been murdered by his own mother. The question was whether she had taken her own life as well. His hands shook as he wrapped the body once again, thinking that the last person to do so had been the child's mother and, and this was the worst of it, convinced that same mother had deliberately killed him, denying him the life that was rightfully his.

'You were right enough. A boy it is.'

'So what are you thinking?'

The two men were sitting drinking strong tea brewed by The Skipper. The dead child remained swaddled on the box bed.

'We need to find out what has happened. It doesn't have the look of an accident. I'll need to get someone over from the town, maybe even from the mainland.' He paused to sip at his tea. 'What are you thinking yourself? You know the sea.'

The Skipper stared at the resurgent flames on the replenished peat fire.

'The poor child wasn't in the sea overlong is what I'm thinking. The sea can do terrible things to a body and the baby is scarce marked.'

'You saw nothing of the mother?'

'Nothing.'

'Could she still be in the water?'

'My, yes. She could be there, alright. Maybe the water will give her up, but it might not.'

'Would it be possible for them to be in the water together and for one to be found and the other lost?'

'My, yes. I'm just thinking that so close to shore, in a storm like last night, she would have been cast up as well.'

'You said you didn't see any sign of a boat?'

'No. And any boat that close to shore last night would have been madness.'

'So how would the baby get into the water?' Constable MacRae was thinking aloud now. 'He didn't fall overboard. So he was either dropped or thrown or placed into the water. And that was done recently. How long would you say at most?'

'I wouldn't have thought it would have been any earlier than late last night. He's so little marked that I can't imagine it was even that long.'

'Come on down to the shore,' said the policeman, finishing his tea. 'Show me where you found him.'

The Skipper drained his own cup and threw the remaining droplets onto the fire, where they sizzled for an instant.

MacRae let him go out first and looked upon the baby's corpse once more before pulling the door behind him. The Skipper was already heading to the shoreline, but stopped short. MacRae followed his stare.

'What is it?'

The old man pointed a gnarled finger at the track at the end of his house leading up to the summer pastures.

'Look at that.'

'What?'

'The track. Somebody has been on it. That wasn't there last night.'

MacRae could see that someone had been slithering up the track, leaving prints clearly embedded in the mud. On one or two imprints, the side had been pushed away where the foot had slipped. There were signs of steps coming the other way, too.

'I was out looking at the sea before the dark,' The Skipper was saying, 'and they weren't there then.'

'Aye, but that could be anyone.'

'Not that I've seen or heard. No one has any beasts on the moor yet to be checking them. And there's no one would have been thinking of fishing last night. These were made this morning.'

'Did you see them when you went to the shore earlier?'

'I did not. But I was staring down at the shore. They could have been there.'

MacRae was looking at them more closely.

'They're smallish feet. They could be a woman's.'

'Aye, but I'm thinking there was more than one of them. Look – that one there is bigger than that one there.'

'So two people went up and two came back.' MacRae stood up abruptly. 'I'll need to get someone over from town. I don't like how this is looking. Can you stay here and make sure no one goes past until I get back? Don't say anything to anyone if they ask. I don't doubt they will.'

'Will the baby be staying here for just now?' The Skipper asked.

The policeman looked at him sympathetically.

'Aye. I think that would be best.'

'Aye,' said the old man.

MacRae turned back towards the village and moved with an urgency that confirmed to those who saw him that something had happened. One of the first faces to see him pass was Annie, watching him through a gap in the door. Her breath was fast and her hands were shaking. There could be no doubt that something had been discovered. She had been in the byre when the two men had passed and she hid, waiting for their return. She had nearly collapsed as the authoritative figure of the policeman come back up the road. There was a relief when he carried on past the house, but she knew that it would only be a temporary.

She almost threw herself back into the living quarters. Mam was seated on her chair, Kirsty curled on the floor at her feet, her head resting on her mother's lap. Mam stroked her daughter's hair in the silence and the warmth, and nothing betrayed the terrible thoughts pulsing through the room.

'Mam!' Annie hissed through gritted teeth.

Her mother looked at her without moving her head.

'Mam. The police have just gone by. Constable MacRae. He was in such a hurry. He must have found something.'

Mam sighed long and deep.

'Mam,' urged Annie with barely suppressed hysteria, 'What are we going to do?'

Mam gazed down at Kirsty and continued to run her hand over her hair.

'There's nothing we can do, girl, nothing we can do at all.'

'But Mam,' Annie implored. 'The police. They might be

coming.'

'So what do we do? Do we run? Do we take this poor, broken child and drag her across the moor? Where would we go? No, my dear, we were possessed by the Devil last night and he made us think wicked thoughts. He made us think that we could deny one of God's own. He had me thinking that I could hide what was my own flesh and blood and give him away; my own flesh and blood. And where has that left us? My daughter killed her own baby and is now broken in spirit and mind. No, we can run no more because the Devil would be leading us and we would have nowhere to go. All we can do is place ourselves before the Lord and beg His forgiveness. And if it is His Will, He will give us the strength to confront whatever lies ahead. There is no other way, lass.'

Annie slid to the floor by the door. She knew what her mother said was true. And so they waited, as the fire smoked and the fates gathered.

At the post office Constable MacRae watched as Peter the Post sent a wire to the police station in town. He had to keep his hand steady as he tapped out the words 'murder suspected'.

9

THEY ARRIVED LATER THAT SAME DAY in a car with solid tyres. Four of them, rattling across the island from town on a road without tarmacadam. Inspector Colin Grant was unhappy. He felt as if he'd been part of a travelling freak show. People had stopped and stared at every village they'd passed through. Children had whooped and yelled and dogs had chased the car, barking and snarling.

Word of mouth travelled more quickly than the automobiles, and could take a more direct line than the meandering road. In districts ahead the alert was out that a car was coming from town with three policemen and a man in a posh coat. It signalled officialdom and frantic attempts were made to hide bottles of illicit alcohol in barns and bothies.

For the last hour though, as they had left the coastal fringes and crossed the interior, they had travelled over bleak moorland, stippled with peat-brown lochs. Some sought such places for solitude, but for the unappreciative soul it was a gloomy, melancholy place. Colin Grant was of no mind to acknowledge the timelessness of the territory.

He wanted to get to his destination quickly. The wire from John MacRae had demanded attention. It had been passed to him and it was to the point. He required assistance; a baby's body had been found, murder was suspected. Murder. It was almost unknown on this island, certainly within living memory. A smuggling operation had brought Grant to the island and, with that inquiry complete, he had expected to sail back to the mainland the next day. But this interested him. He had heard older colleagues in Inverness speak casually of infanticide. It was a warped world, he thought, that placed more on community acceptance than on the life of a newborn baby. But those same colleagues had never condemned, finding too often that the mother was a girl demented by panic or a woman confronted with dividing what little there was into even smaller portions. Who could be judge? Grant had been troubled by that view. He wondered who spoke for the child. Perhaps, he thought, this case might allow him a clearer understanding. His quest for that understanding, though, was being sorely tested by the bumping, jarring, rolling drive. At least the rain had gone.

'Have we much further to go?' he asked tetchily.

'About two miles,' replied Sergeant MacArthur, sitting in the front, beside the driver.

'MacRae's a good man, you say? This won't be a waste of time?'

'No sir. MacRae is sound,' the Sergeant answered, for the third time. 'As I say, sir, he never really has any bother over here.'

Grant's agitation grew as yet another jolt bumped his hat off the roof of the car. He was set for abandoning it and walking the rest of the way when they passed the first isolated house that signposted the imminence of a township.

More blackhouses passed, closer together now and so natural set against the moor. Then the Sergeant announced their arrival and they pulled up alongside a white cottage.

A throng of children gathered round to touch the car. Feet, carts and beasts were the usual modes of transport, although trucks and vans were becoming more familiar. A car, though, an automobile, that was a rarity. The children were hypnotised by the chrome and the engine. The driver got out to shoo them away.

Grant climbed out and stretched, his grey coat riding up on his shoulders, and he stretched his legs with each step as he followed the Sergeant to the door, giving him an unusual gait. The Sergeant was already coming back to the car.

'We've to go on down to end of the village. That's where he is.'

Grant looked back at the car.

'I don't have to travel in that damned thing again, do I?'

'Either that, or walk a couple of miles.'

'I'll walk. Where am I going?'

'I'll come with you, sir.'

Inspector Grant, Sergeant MacArthur and the Constable who

had travelled over with them began to walk through the village. The driver waited behind with the car and a welcome cup of tea from Mary MacRae.

The walk gave Grant the chance to see the village and the villagers, to get a gut feeling of any underlying tensions. There was none. There was certainly interest in the entourage. People stared, as was their way, and one or two nodded a greeting. There was curiosity, but nothing more. He knew that rumour would already be rife. Whether or not they knew what had happened. But there was no hostility, no closing of ranks against the strangers.

Most of the people of the Highlands lived in such places and he'd seen many of them. They were almost invariably coastal settlements, the straths of the interior having been cleared long since. The people had worked hard on their land, had broken rock and teased crops to grow in scant patches of earth. The church was the focal point, even more so here on the islands. But for all the holiness and respectability he knew that crime and sin could thrive here as well as anywhere. The savage, gratuitous crime of the cities was uncommon and doors need not be locked, but passions and envy and malice simmered, here, as anywhere.

'What d'you know of this place?' Grant asked MacArthur.

'Much the same as the rest of the island, sir. A bit remote from the town, but much the same as anywhere else. The people go to church and get on with their lives.'

'And there's never been anything out of the ordinary, nothing odd?'

'Not that I know of, sir. MacRae would have a better idea, right enough.'

Grant could hear the sea as they came round a horseshoe bend in the road. Soon he saw Constable MacRae, standing outside the last house in the village. The Constable stiffened himself, straightening to his full height of over six feet. He towered over Grant.

'Constable MacRae?'

'Yes sir.'

'I'm Inspector Grant, this is Sergeant MacArthur and Constable Smith. What have you got to tell us?'

'There is the body of a baby in the house here, sir. The man who lives here found him floating on the tide this morning.'

'Your wire suggests you suspect murder?'

'That's my impression, sir.'

'Why?'

'Well, as I say, the child had not been in the sea overlong. There's no trace of his mother and there's no sign of any boat having been near. I can't see how else he got into the water.'

'Is it possible the mother is still in the water?'

'It could be, but The Skipper reckons she would have been washed up too. The Skipper knows the sea and this part of the coast, sir. Also, there were fresh footprints on the tracks up to the cliffs this morning. I don't like the look of it.'

'What does the doctor think?'

'He confirmed the child was dead, sir. He said we'd need a post mortem to be sure, but it looks like a drowning.'

'That would mean it wasn't a still birth?'

'That's what the doctor said, sir.'

'Are the remains in here?'

'Yes sir.'

MacRae led the way into The Skipper's house. The old man was sitting in his chair by the fire. Grant squinted his eyes in the gloom. The local policeman made cursory introductions. The Skipper remained in his chair and nodded to each of the newcomers.

'The remains are here, sir.'

Grant stepped across to look and was silent for a few moments.

'The doctor's arranging to take him over to town, sir,' MacRae said, 'but I thought it better to leave him here until you saw him.'

Grant nodded, turned his face to The Skipper and asked him to go through his story again.

'I'll show you,' said the old man.

The Skipper and MacRae took him to the shore indicating the track leading to the cliffs. The footprints were fainter, but still distinct. Grant looked about him, struck by the drama of the rising cliffs.

'You think he was thrown from up there?'

'Possibly. That's where the tracks seem to lead,' said MacRae.

'I'd have thought he'd have been more marked than he was if he'd been thrown from there.'

'The wind last night was a strong one,' explained The Skipper. 'Some gusts could have lifted a man as big as the Constable here off his feet. A wee thing like that? It would almost have flown. Like as not he never even touched the cliffs before hitting the water.'

The Skipper led them round to the north side of the shore and pointed to where he'd taken the wretched bundle from the water. It was an austere and foreboding place, with the cliffs rising sheer above them. Further out, caves had been bored into the rock face and where they were closer to the shore there were serrations that in some far future time would penetrate right through, unless the overhang collapsed first. It provided cover from the wind, but they could hear their voices now echo eerily, with the intermittent squeal of a seabird. Here the sea clanked against the fallen boulders, but the water on which the froth floated seemed unable to return from these pools and swirls and swells. It was such a lifeless place, so close to the vigour of the open bay, but scarce touched by the sun or the wind.

'This is where the sea comes to die,' The Skipper said without drama. 'See how once the water comes in here, it's trapped until the tide goes back and it can drain away. That's what happened to the child. It would just have risen and fallen on the swell.'

'It's good you found him when you did, Skipper. It's a God-forsaken place.'

The three men returned to the shoreline.

'The Sergeant tells me they're all God-fearing people here.'

'Yes sir.'

'I've little doubt that this will be straightforward, but you know this place, MacRae. There's nothing unusual going on that would explain it? No dervishes dancing at the moon, that sort of thing?'

MacRae looked perplexed and almost sniffed in laughter.

'No sir.'

'It's not as daft as it sounds. It wouldn't be the first time, even in a place as quiet as this.'

'No sir,' MacRae answered emphatically. 'There's nothing like that here. The only worshipping is at the Christian church, sir.'

'The only devil they might worship,' The Skipper interjected with jarring levity, 'is the whisky.'

'So what are your thoughts, MacRae?' Grant asked.

'Somebody didn't want the baby, sir. It could only be a young girl. Maybe her mother.'

'She should be easy enough to find, shouldn't she?'

'You would think, sir. The doctor doesn't know of any births expected just now. There's been no word of any girl expecting. No one's gone missing. There's been nothing.'

'Has word got out?'

'They'll know something is happening, but probably not what. The Skipper says he's told no one, but the postman saw the wire.'

'We'll need to start calling at houses, but first let's have a look up there,' said Grant, looking up to the cliffs.

They scrabbled back up the shoreline and onto the track, Grant sweating and panting slightly in his overcoat, hating to be outdone by the old, oil-skinned man. They examined the footprints on the trail to the pastures. There was little doubt from their size that they were not a man's. MacRae, with his longer legs, stepped over them, and then pulled both The Skipper and Grant up behind him. By the time Grant was level with him, The Skipper was already yards ahead.

'Who would come up here?' Grant asked MacRae a little breathlessly.

'Mostly sheep. Some of the crofters use it as a shortcut to the summer pastures. I've used it myself once or twice for the fishing.'

'Fishing?'

'There's some fine rock fishing to be had from the cliffs.'

The Skipper stood above them at the crest of the path, looking along the cliff tops, his white whiskers tugged tight by the wind. Grant, panting now, looked up at him with some irritation because this fit old man was exposing his own lack of stamina. When he too reached the top, he removed his tight bowler hat and felt the chill of the wind against the perspiration in his hair. His polished boots were stained by mud and sheep droppings and he reproached himself for not being better prepared. He'd been on the islands often enough to know that dressing for the weather and land made more sense than dressing for appearance.

'This is one hell of a climb for a woman who's just given birth. Someone else must have been involved,' Grant puffed.

'The body can find strength when it needs to,' said The Skipper matter-of-factly.

MacRae looked down upon the houses packed close together at this end of the road before they wound round the Horseshoe and were lost from sight. They could be seen again further on where the road rose with the landscape and the houses were strung out with greater distance between them. Something had been niggling at his memory ever since The Skipper had come to him, something distracting at the back of his mind that he felt he should remember. As he scanned the village his eyes paused over the MacLeod house. Then it struck him, the incident involving the daughter, Kirsty, back at the time of the Road Dance. At the time he had suspected there was more to it, but the girl had told him nothing. He remembered her withdrawn attitude, so defensive for someone who claimed only to have fallen. He had considered many possibilities at the time; maybe she had drunk too much, or had been carrying on with the boys, but there was still something that bothered him. She had not deviated from her story and there had been nothing more he could do without her acquiescence. He had seen her about since, but she had appeared to be as ever she was, and the episode had faded. How long ago was it? When the boys left for the Front? About nine months ago? Yes. Nine months. He was at once sure and saddened.

The Skipper was already hastening along the cliff in his deceptively fast shuffle, repeatedly looking down to the sea. Grant was striding to keep just behind him, his arms jerking out at sharp angles to keep his balance on the treacherously wet grass. MacRae glanced back at the MacLeod house again before following them. There would be time enough to call.

'What exactly are you looking for?' Grant called after The Skipper. He was prepared to be led by the old man and use his intimate knowledge of the area and environment.

'To see where she threw the baby from.'

'How will you know? We seem to have lost any tracks.'

'Look for the sheer drops.'

MacRae was now just behind Grant.

'It's all bloody sheer,' muttered the Inspector.

The Skipper was soon two hundred yards ahead of the policemen. Where the cliff top had given way and collapsed to the sea he sure-footedly sidled along the ridges that had formed where the soil had subsided, but not fallen away. Grant was aghast, one slip or foot in the wrong place and the old man would have tumbled onto the rocks below. Both he and MacRae took detours around these gashes.

At length they could see The Skipper had stopped and, having peered over the cliff edge, was now staring all around him. He had reached the outermost point of the bay where the cliffs swept round to follow the coastline north. There was no more land before them. Here the only growth were scrapings in the fissures of the rock and small spreads of grass in some leeward crevices.

'I think she would have come to here,' stated The Skipper.

'Why?'

'It would have gone straight into the sea. It wouldn't have hit any rocks. Just straight in.'

'Why would that matter to her?' MacRae asked this time.

'That I couldn't tell you. But you saw the child. Scarce a mark upon him. He went straight into the sea. Maybe she thought if she came out this far he would be carried out to the ocean. She didn't read the tide.'

It was the longest either of the policemen had heard The Skipper speak.

'Maybe she just wasn't thinking at all,' he concluded, almost to himself.

Grant examined the ground around them, but there was nothing to see. There was insufficient soil for a footprint, too much rain had fallen to leave any mark on the rocks and anything dropped or torn would have been long gone in the wind.

The three men then stood silently looking down at the rise and fall of the water far below. Inspector Grant had seen much in his time, been in rooms of death and looked down upon grotesquely savaged bodies, but nothing had chilled him as this. There was nothing to see, no gore or carnage, just the flintiness of the rock, the swell of the sea, the push of the wind and the knowledge that from here a mother had thrown her own child to his certain death, only hours before. What could have driven her to that? The anger he had felt towards her when he saw the baby's remains had gone. From this vantage point he knew she had not been of sound mind. What fear had so deranged her? What horrors must be with her now? If, indeed, she was still alive.

'From here,' he observed, 'it's hard to believe she didn't throw herself.'

'We'll know soon enough,' said MacRae.

They turned their backs to the ocean and retraced their steps towards the village, finding it easier now with the wind at their backs. At intervals they thought they could maybe see a print, but always indistinct, never certain.

They walked with their own thoughts: Grant considered how best to conduct a search of the village and arrange the removal of the remains to the town for a post mortem; MacRae wanted to be certain of his facts before confronting the MacLeods; and The Skipper felt a depth of sadness he had little known in his long life, a life throughout which sorrow had always been a breath away.

As they came off the moor and onto the road, Grant again took command.

'I'll arrange for transport to remove the remains as soon as we get back to the police house,' he said to The Skipper. 'In the meantime, if you have no objections, I would like to leave him where he is. I'm sure you understand.'

'I've sat with bodies for longer than that. You do what you need to do,' said the old man.

Grant instructed the Constable from town to remain at The Skipper's house and he, MacRae and the Sergeant began the walk back to the police house. MacRae saw faces in doorways, saying nothing, but asking everything with their expressions. As he passed the MacLeods' house there was nothing, no movement, no sound; but for the curl of blue smoke from the opening in the thatch of the roof, no sign of life either. His every instinct told him to go to the house now, but he had to be sure first.

'Whoever did this can't have gone far,' Grant was saying. 'If someone has disappeared suddenly, we'll know. And if they haven't, then we'll see them as we go round.'

The walk back to the police house was brisk. MacRae kept quiet, responding to direct questions, but otherwise clarifying his own thoughts. At the house, as the Inspector accepted a cup of tea and told the two other policemen what he wanted done, MacRae took a notebook from a locked cupboard. He flicked through the pages of his own tightly-written copperplate script. It didn't take long to find the note he had made of visiting Kirsty MacLeod. It had been eight months, three weeks and four days previously. There could be little doubt.

'Inspector.'

The chatting stopped. The tone of MacRae's voice insisted upon it.

'Inspector, I think I know what happened.'

Grant swallowed a mouthful of sweet tea and waited for MacRae to continue.

'Almost nine months ago a girl in the village was hurt at a dance here. I'd heard that she been hurt quite badly, sir, and I went to see her. She told me that she'd tripped and hit her head against a rock. She wouldn't say any more, but I was sure she was hiding something. There wasn't much more I could do, though, if she wasn't going to tell me what had happened. I told her if she wanted to speak to me, I would listen. I've heard nothing from her. And now this.'

Grant slurped another mouthful of tea, the sound of his swallowing loud in the silence.

'You think the baby could be hers?'

'I don't know for sure, but it would tie in. Surely the doctor would know.'

Doctor MacLean sat at home, a large whisky in his hand. He had seen dead children before, too often. He had watched little babies battle for life, willed them to make it and done everything he could do. When it wasn't enough and another baby had died and another mother had cried. It was the way of things. Although he was affected by every single one, there was an extent to which he was inured.

This one had juddered him. Not immediately. There hadn't been an instant flinching, but as he learned about the circumstances of its discovery and counted back the months, he had reached the same conclusions as Constable MacRae. He remembered Kirsty MacLeod that night. He had known what had happened. He should have done more to help her. He hadn't. He could hide behind the fact that she did not want his help, but that's all he'd been doing, hiding. He should have returned to her, counselled her and been there for her and he never was. And it had come to this, a dead baby and a shattered girl. The responsibility weighed heavily upon him and he had again turned to the whisky to ease the burden. All it did was paralyse him, and he sat and he brooded.

He didn't even hear the door knock. His wife pushed open the door to the living room and ushered the policemen in.

'He's in here,' she said, addressing to MacRae and ignoring her husband.

The two policemen nodded their thanks and came into the room. The doctor took some moments to register their presence. His glass lay on the floor beside his chair and neither of the visitors saw it, but they didn't need to. They could smell alcohol around him and see it in his manner. It made them hesitate.

'John,' said MacRae eventually, 'this is Inspector Colin Grant.'

The two men looked at each other and the doctor visibly pulled himself together.

'I'm sorry, gentleman,' he said with a forced professionalism. 'I was almost dozing.'

'We need your help,' Grant explained. 'Constable MacRae says he thinks he might know who the mother of the baby is. We're going to see her now, and I'd be grateful if you would come with us.'

The doctor trembled again. Good God, so soon! They would have come to her eventually. He had known that, but he had expected that he would have had time to see her and to prepare her. Not now.

'I think it's Kirsty MacLeod.' MacRae sounded both solemn

and sad. 'You remember the night of the Road Dance? Kirsty was hurt that night. Remember? We spoke about it. I think something more serious happened and I have a feeling this is the end of it.'

'She never said anything to me, if that's what you're asking.'

'No, but you were concerned, yourself, at the time. You suggested yourself that I should see her.'

'Yes. Yes, I did, didn't I.'

'If Constable MacRae is right,' Grant interjected, 'then we can sort this out quickly and get the girl whatever help she needs. And it won't be hanging over the community.'

'Oh, this will hang over them,' thought the doctor, with bitter certainty. 'This will hang over them for years to come.'

The village was in a frenzy of rumour. Something significant was happening. Strangers were in their midst, aliens in their village intent on business about which they knew nothing. Such earnestness to know what was happening allowed some stories to be taken as truly as if they'd been written in the Good Book.

'The Germans have tried to land. They were going to use the island as a back door to the mainland.' It was only the failure of any mad dash of soldiers to the village that snared that story.

'They're chasing a spy. One of these German agents came ashore in the storm. The Skipper saw him.' Byres were checked and horizons scanned for the elusive agent. The Skipper had a procession of visitors, none of whom he let into his house.

'I can't tell you anything. You'll know soon enough.' The enigmatic message he sent out fuelled the conspiracies all the more. None of them could have guessed the truth, that a baby, one of their own, had been killed in their own bay. That would have been too terrible.

There was no such energy in the MacLeod house. Behind their doors there was silence. Kirsty cowered in her bed, where only hours before her baby had been born. The birth sheets had been taken off and fresh ones put in their place. Mam sat beside her, rocking from the waist, with a Bible open in her lap. Kirsty's eyes were closed and her breath was shallow, but even. Annie had boiled water and was soaking the sheets in the tin bath. No one spoke. The clock ticked on.

Outside there was clatter of hooves on stone and the rattling of metal and wood. It was the cart on its way to The Skipper's house. Only Annie heard it stop outside their own house. She heard the thud and clatter of people getting off it and the low mumble of their voices before the jolting of the horse and cart began again on the remaining few yards to The Skipper's house. She quivered suddenly and violently. She stopped pounding the sheets in the bath and waited for the inevitable. The scrunch of the feet outside seemed to take an age. Her eyes bore at the door, waiting. Even so, when the door was rapped it took her by surprise. She clasped her hands, but her arms, shoulders and body continued to tremble.

'That will be them, then.'

Mam's voice was quietly resigned.

'Open the door, lass.'

'Oh Mam...'

'Open the door. Let them in.'

Annie's legs could hardly support her as she moved to the door. She pulled at the handle and opened it to a crack. Three men stood there. Constable MacRae at the front, Dr MacLean at his shoulder and level with him a smaller man with a bowler hat and large moustache.

'Annie,' MacRae said, 'Is your mother in?'

Without a word she pulled the door back to let them in. The sense of fear was palpable. MacRae stepped past her followed by the other two men, each removing their hat as they entered. Mam was standing with her hand resting on the dresser.

'Mrs MacLeod. You know the doctor, and this is Inspector Grant.'

Mam looked along the faces before her.

MacRae glanced down at the hat he'd taken off and rubbed his finger along the police crest.

'Is Mr MacLeod at home?'

She shook her head.

'We need to speak to Kirsty. Is she at home?'

Grant's eyes were darting about the room. There was no one else in the room, but he noticed the washing in the bath and the girl who'd let them in still standing rigidly with her back against the door. There was little doubt MacRae was right. Something hung heavily in the atmosphere.

'Do you know why we're here?' MacRae was asking.

'Yes,' Mam replied softly and nodded towards the adjoining room. 'Kirsty is in her bed.'

'Can we see her?'

Mam lowered her head in acquiescence.

'The doctor would like to see her first to check her. Then Inspector Grant would like to speak to her.'

Doctor MacLean, carrying his leather bag, sidled past MacRae.

'You understand that I am only interested in her medical well-being?' he said to Mam. She barely nodded. He went through to the bedroom, leaving the four remaining static.

He could see her eyes glisten in the gloom, staring straight at him, like a frightened, cornered animal. She had heard the voices. She knew they had come for her. MacLean hated himself for having let this happen.

'Kirsty, it's me. Doctor MacLean.'

There was no response, not even a blink. He put his hat on the other bed in the room and pulled off his overcoat. Her eyes followed him. He sat down at the foot of her bed and rested his elbows on his knees. Her mind cranked and she recalled him adopting the same pose that awful night of the Road Dance when she had been taken to his house.

'Kirsty, the police are here. Constable MacRae and a detective from the mainland. They want to speak to you.' He raised his head to look at her. 'Is there anything you want to tell me before they come in?'

She lay still and said nothing.

'Kirsty, no one wants to hurt you. Talk to me.'

There was nothing.

'I need to look at you. I need to examine you. Whatever has happened, Kirsty, I need to make sure you are alright. Will you let me look at you?'

And still she did not move.

MacLean stood up slowly and stepped to the head of the bed.

Her eyes never left his. He kneeled down bringing his head level to hers, put his arm on the bed and rested his chin upon it. She was lying on her back and turned her head to him, the first movement she had made since he'd entered the room.

'Whatever happens,' he whispered, 'I want to help you through it. I know what happened at the Road Dance. I think I know what has happened since. If you trust me I can help you. God alone knows why you should, but you need help.'

She smelt the alcohol on his breath and held his eyes. He felt as if she was staring deep into his soul.

He continued whispering, only the hard consonants actually making any sound. He spoke haltingly, pausing at length between each sentence as if sure of what he wanted to say, but not so certain of how to say it.

'The baby looked to be asleep, just asleep. There wasn't a mark on him. I think he is in a better place. I think you did what you did because you loved him so much. You did what you thought was right. I won't condemn you for that; no one would. You can tell them what you want and I won't pass on any of it. I just want to make sure that you have not been... you've not been damaged.'

He slipped his left hand beneath the covers and slowly pulled them back. She did not resist, did not try to hold them to her as a pathetic protection.

'Can you pull up your nightdress, or shall I?'

He had to do it himself. He had to push his arm under the small of her back to lift her hips, using his other hand to pull down her pants. A thick pad of cloth had been placed between her legs, just as he had done almost nine months before. He closed his eyes, hoping that she had not done this all alone, that some one had been there to help her, even if he had not.

His professional eye told him that the birth had been difficult, but there was no lasting damage. He took what he needed from his bag to stitch the wound. It was difficult working in the light that came from the small window set in the roof, but he wanted to make as good a job as he could. He had failed her and now wanted to do right by her. Once she issued a short, high pitched squeak, but otherwise she was stoic.

When it was over, Kirsty lay like a heavy rag doll. MacLean vigorously rubbed his hands on a towel that had been draped at the foot of the bed. What agonies had she endured in this room only hours before?

She felt his hands pressing around her lower abdomen, ensuring that nothing had been left inside her. It was as if she was out of herself and the examination was happening to someone else. How often had she felt that, in the past months? The doctor was gentle with her, but there was a set grimness about him. And there was the smell of the alcohol.

He smoothed her nightdress back down and pulled the blankets back over her, tucking her in as if she were a little girl. As he looked on her, gravity pulled down what little flesh there was in his face and gave him a slightly puffy appearance. He kissed her on the forehead and she heard him sniff back a tear.

'Kirsty, I'm not going to let them see you. You need to rest.' The doctor stood up. 'I want you to trust me and I will do the best I can for you.'

He put on his coat and picked up his hat and bag.

'I'll come back to you.'

With that he was gone.

Kirsty turned her head to face the ceiling. Her eyes gazed at the thatch above her and the faint smell of him lingered around her.

In the living room it appeared as if there had been no conversation. Mam had supplied the men with cups of tea and they were both now sitting. Annie remained standing at the door. There was a gentle whizzing sound and then the chords of the clock rang out the quarter hour.

MacRae and Grant stood up expectantly as the doctor came back in. MacLean nodded at Mam.

'She'll be alright,' he said, then beckoned to the two policemen to follow him outside. They both looked surprised, but did as they were bade. Annie pushed herself further back against the door, but none of the men looked at her as they stepped outside.

'What is it?' Grant asked as soon as they were out of earshot of the house.

'I don't think you should speak to her.'

'Is she alright?' MacRae asked, genuine concern in his voice.

'Yes.'

'Why can't we speak to her then?' Grant was impatient.

'Because I don't think she did it.'

'That's all very well, doctor, but if you'll forgive me, I am the detective. I will decide whether she did it or not. I will bow to your medical expertise, but...'

'She didn't do it, because she's never had a baby.'

Doctor MacLean's interruption left the policemen aghast.

'That's right, gentlemen,' he said. 'The girl in there has never given birth.'

10

'YOU ARE SURE there is no mistake?' It was the third time the detective had asked the question in the short walk back from Kirsty's house to The Skipper's.

'Quite sure. Get a second opinion if you want, but any doctor will only tell you what I have.'

Grant's voice was a monotone, but not flat. He was clamping his anger and only his lips moved.

'You saw them in that house, doctor. Something was wrong. They'd been waiting for us. Believe me, I know when I'm expected. I can feel it. And they were expecting us.'

'The girl had never given birth, Inspector,' said Dr MacLean, controlling his delivery to conceal his nervousness. There was tension between the two men, who stood barely a pace apart.

Grant's voice began to rise.

'The girl was hidden away, for Christ's sake. Why do that if there was nothing wrong?'

'She was upset.'

'What could make her so upset that she was hidden away from us?'

'Because her young man is dead.'

Grant was taken aback.

The doctor saw his gamble might work. MacRae was also looking hard at him now.

'Her beau. He was one of those killed at the Front. She only heard the news yesterday and she's been in her bed since. Did her mother not say?'

'No she did not. She said nothing at all.'

'They're all in shock.'

Grant absorbed this.

'The mother said nothing,' he repeated. 'Not a word. But I'll tell you one thing, she wasn't surprised to see us. Why would that be?'

'I don't know. These are simple people. Maybe after the news of the boy they weren't surprised to see someone in authority. I don't know.'

'So whose baby was that, and who killed it?'

There was no answer. He hadn't expected one.

MacRae was at a complete loss.

'What do we do now sir?' he asked.

'We do it the hard way, Constable. We call at every house and find out what people know, what they have seen. A child can't just be born and nobody knows or cares about it. Somebody must have seen something. And the house we are going to start at is the house we've just left.'

Grant saw the doctor look sharply at him.

'I know what you've said, doctor, and I'll keep it in mind. But whoever did this had to pass these houses to get onto the cliffs. Somebody in that house may have heard something. It is not unreasonable to go back.'

'There is a great deal of distress in there, Inspector. Throughout the whole village in fact. Three boys have been killed and hardly a house has been unaffected. You must have seen that.'

'I've got a job to do here, doctor, and I intend to do it.'

'I understand that, but perhaps it would be better to wait until after tonight's service.'

'What service?'

'There is to be a service of mourning at the church tonight. Let them get that out of the way. Let them come to terms with what's happened first.'

'I need to move quickly, doctor. The longer I leave it, the more chance of whoever killed that baby getting away.'

But the doctor would not give up.

'Inspector. We don't know that anyone killed that baby. It may have been stillborn. And I have told you that I know of no one in this district who was expecting a child now. There are women in various stages, but none that was due now. That baby was a full term birth. If the mother was from here, I'll find out soon enough. She is going to need help or we're going to hear that she's disappeared. Everything seems to suggest she wasn't from here anyway. Why cause more distress in these homes?'

The Inspector pondered.

'What d'you think, Constable? You know the place, the people.'

MacRae looked past Grant, pulling his thoughts into a coherent sequence.

'I'm inclined to agree with the doctor sir. I'm not sure how much you'd get. There is real shock over what happened to the boys and people have been calling at the houses of their families to pay their respects. It's not been like normal when everything is noticed.'

'So you'd wait until tomorrow, until this service is passed?'

'I would, sir.'

Grant took off his hat and rubbed his hand across his face in resignation.

'Very well,' he sighed. 'First we must take the remains of the poor child over to town for a post mortem. I want to know if he was dead before he was in the water.'

The Constable from town was despatched back through the village to bring a horse and cart to The Skipper's house. Grant and MacRae returned to the shore and walked up the path to the cliffs again, to be sure that they had missed nothing. Dr MacLean went back into The Skipper's house and found the old seaman sitting next to the body of the baby, murmuring passages from the Bible.

When the doctor came in, the old man gently closed the book, got off the chair with a slight sigh and stepped across the room. There he stood, his Bible in his hands.

The doctor looked down on the dead child. The eyes were half closed and the mouth partially opened. The beginnings of expression, the doctor thought. He looked at the child, wondering what he should do.

'Take the sheet,' said The Skipper quietly. 'You'll need to cover him.'

'Yes, yes,' said Dr MacLean absently. 'Thank you.'

He pulled up the corners of the blanket and began to fold one side over the body.

'It'll come loose if you do that,' said The Skipper. 'You lift him and I'll fold the sheet.'

The doctor scooped the body from the wet towel that had been the child's death robe, pulled it to him and straightened up. It was so light he could have lifted him with one hand. He held him close, supporting the head with the crook of his elbow and the torso with the length of his forearm, and he gazed down upon him as if he were his own.

The Skipper folded the blanket in half, then folded it again, and nodded to the doctor to put the body back down on it. Then he wound it snugly around the child, until only a corner flap was left which would cover the face. The doctor wondered why the old man was so deft. Perhaps he had done this before at sea when the bodies could not be carried home. As he made to cover the child completely, Dr MacLean grasped his arm, placed two fingers against his own lips and softly touched them against the baby's forehead. When he was done, the Skipper tucked the final fold and the face and form of the child was gone. The two men stood together and the older one murmured a prayer.

Then the doctor turned abruptly and left The Skipper's house. Outside he walked to edge of the grey wall and looked up to the cliffs, scanning for the figures of the policemen. There was no sign of them. Quickly, he returned to the house of the three women.

The box was carried to the cart in the outstretched arms of the doctor. Once it had carried tea half way across the world from India. Now it was the body of a baby being taken from a place that never knew him. A loose knot of locals had gathered.

The significance of the box was lost on them, but death hung over the scene like a shroud. They saw the barely recognisable figure of The Skipper, unfamiliar because he had removed his cap. They saw the skin stretched over his skull and a few strands of white hair weaving in the wind. The two uniformed police officers also stood bareheaded.

Death had visited The Skipper's house, although no one but himself stayed there. Whatever was being mourned was in the box being carried by the doctor. And why was the doctor here?

And the policemen from town?

As Dr MacLean reached the cart, the policeman swung himself up onto it, lifted the box from the doctor and placed it at the back. He had to use both arms, not for the weight, but because of the dimensions of the box. Inside he could see white sheet wrapped tightly in a small bundle.

Nothing had been said since the men had emerged from the house. The Skipper stood at his doorway, his black hat clasped in both his hands in front of him. With a flick of the reins, a clatter of hooves and the rattle of the steel-rimmed wheels on the stones of the road the horse pulled the gig around to face back up the village road. All the figures on it jerked backwards in unison as the gig jolted forward.

As they passed the MacLeod house, Mam watched through a crack in the door. Her grandson was taken away, away from everything that he should have been a part of. Tears coursed down her face. How could she have let it come to this? When her Kirsty had needed support and guidance she had failed her, she had been so consumed by the dread of what others would think. This was the result; a baby, her own grandson, dead and her daughter's mind broken. As the cart and its tragic cargo rattled on towards the Horseshoe bend, Mam knew with dreadful certainty that it was not over yet. As long as her daughter lived, it never would be.

Three silences marked the journey though the village: the doctor nervous and uncomfortable; Inspector Grant breathing through his nose deeply and often and seemingly struggling to be quiet; behind him there was the unknown soundlessness of Constable MacRae.

The gig's course along the village road was marked by people staring through half open doors. Few noticed the box, but they saw the men and could not miss their grimness. When they arrived at MacRae's cottage, the passengers jumped down. The Constable clambered over the back of the cart and lifted the box down to MacRae, who carried it over to the car and placed it on the back seat.

Grant instructed the driver.

'Take this straight back to town and up to the hospital, you understand? It has to be done soonest. Wire me with the result of the post mortem and when Dr Connolly is on his way. Ask him to bring the full report with him.'

'Yes sir'

'Right officer, on you go.'

The policeman started up the car, which vibrated loudly as the engine turned over. Then he released the handbrake and turned on to the stone road. The remains of the baby never returned and it was as if he had never existed.

After the wagon had gone the house and all around it was silent. Kirsty was sleeping.

'I must go the Church tonight,' Mam said quietly.

Annie looked at her sharply.

'I must. How can I not?'

'But Mam,' Annie pleaded.

'The doctor said it would be best if we went. You heard him yourself. That Inspector will be back and he'll be back all the sooner if he thinks we're hiding. The whole village will be there tonight, even those poor mothers who have lost their boys. How will it look if I'm not there?'

'Mam, you can't,' Annie responded urgently. 'Kirsty can't go anywhere and you can't leave me here with her on my own. I don't know that she wouldn't have thrown herself in if I hadn't found her.'

'We have to be strong. The doctor says that it will pass if we act right.'

'Oh Mam, I'm so scared.'

'There's nothing else we can do, dear. If Kirsty is taken from us what will happen to her then? I was weak. I've got to do what I can for her now. They will find out if they are meant to.'

The afternoon wore on with the tick of the clock and the crackle of the flame. Mam sat the whole time with Kirsty who slept deeply, but restlessly. The doctor had told her that Kirsty must not be allowed to leave her bed. He'd assured her that physically there was no cause to be concerned, but he could not guess the damage to her mind. He said he would return when he could.

Evening came. Mam put on her black hat and coat. No words passed between her and Annie until she was ready to leave.

'Just sit with her, lass, until I come home.'

As Mam left into the smir outside, others were already making their way to the church. She would join them and walk with them and talk of the tragedies of the day, all the while keeping her own personal torment to herself.

The church was a sombre, sorrowful place that evening. None of the chatter or greetings of folk arriving for a regular service. Only grim nods of acknowledgement and the stifled sobs. All was black: the hats, the coats and the thoughts.

Grant sat at the back of the hall. He was not much of a believer. He had seen too much, sloshed through too many human sewers where God's light did not shine. But at times like this he wondered. These people knew the only constants in life were the land, the sky and their God. All else was changeable, nothing was forever. For generations their lives and fate had been bound by powers beyond them. It was a life exposed to the forces of nature without distraction or protection. And it was with that clarity that they believed in the Almighty. In its own way the potency of that faith was as strong as the natural energy that forged it.

He was a hard man, was Grant. He had been on the beat in the Glasgow slums and ports further down the Clyde. You had to be tough, and the dividing line between the thugs and the police themselves was sometimes a thin one. It was the way it had to be and it left his heart scarred with cynicism, aggression and contempt. But he was moved by the palpable misery within this small church where the bereaved sought solace from the God who had taken their boys from them.

In all the bowed heads there were images of young lads; sons, brothers, grandchildren. Of shy lovers and friends. There was such sadness for the lives cut short and trepidation for futures without them. For three women in particular the common belief that dying soldiers cried out for their mothers was an anguish too much to bear.

The chief elder, the leather of his boots creaking, climbed wearily to the pulpit, where he placed a large leather-bound, Bible down with a thump. He descended again, holding the rail for support, and joined the other elders on a dais around the pulpit. He moved through the familiar ritual lost in his own thoughts. His grandson was one of those who had died so far from home.

Reverend MacIver followed presently, his head bowed, praying that God might give him the power to comfort the bereaved. When he had visited the homes he had listened as the pain had burst forth from the bereaved and he had responded instinctively. Now though he had to speak and to guide, not just those who had lost, but to others seeking direction. He had sought it himself after leaving the homes of the grieving. He had prayed hard, scoured his Bible, read old notes and knew that nothing he could say would make any difference. There had been sorrowful services before, terrible times when fishermen had been lost at sea. But there had been nothing like this.

They sang from the Psalms of David, Psalm 116. Some in the congregation could not. They were there to listen for something that might give them hope for their lost ones. Others filled their chests and made their voices loud, keeping their emotions at bay. Then the minister prayed long and hesitantly, his mind moving ahead to what he might say.

There would be no eulogy, it was not the way of this church, but there had to be meaning to such loss.

War, he told them, would end when the Gospel prevailed. The Lord had placed his only Son on this earth to bring peace. But man was slow to change and must endure the waste of war. Only by recognising this could man come to the joy of accepting the Lord. Not that the Empire, or indeed these brave lads, had sued for war. Right was with them. They had fought and died for King and Country and for God. Theirs would be the Glory.

'In the Psalms, we sang of the death of the saints being precious in the life of the Lord. And so it is with the boys we have lost. Their suffering is over and we need pity them no more. The pity is with those who remain.'

Death, he told them, was the result of sin. But for the people of God, death was a weapon of destruction against sin, and it gave liberty from the powers of darkness.

Some heads nodded in comprehension, other eyes held his face, not understanding exactly, but at least drawing strength from one they thought so wise telling them that the lost boys were not lost forever. Other heads remained bowed, his words flying over them, unable to lift their grief. By the sermon's end, when they stood for the final prayer, the Reverend MacIver felt that he had done what he could. It didn't end this night, that much he knew, but he believed truly that he had made some connections.

Grant was wondering why he had come. The misery of the place was stifling. Guilt might be hiding in this congregation, there would have been no way to tell. All was sadness, and whispered words and cast down faces.

Grant left the church first and stood well back. One of the first to emerge was Mrs MacLeod. She waited for no one made straight for home without stopping to talk to anyone. Her daughters would still be at home. Hiding, Grant thought, then reproached himself for his reflexive cynicism. The doctor had said to him the girl had never had a child. Why should he doubt him? But doubt he did. It was hard to believe that the homely figure rushing away down the road could been part of anything so wrong. She could have been his own mother. But when everything was at stake, even the righteous could be dragged down the darkest tracks into sin unknown. He would be back at the MacLeods' tomorrow.

He watched a woman walk out of the church supported by her husband and a large-boned youth. Her left hand damping at her red, fleshy face with a hanky. The man focused himself on being strong for her. The teenager looked bewildered and ungainly, unsure of what he was to do and why this was happening. Grant felt like a trespasser. There would be nothing for him to see here, but he waited until they had all dispersed, like the ebbing sea slipping back down the shore. Then he walked the short distance to the police cottage.

Annie jolted awake. The silence and warmth had wrapped around her on the chair, lulling her to sleep. She looked to find Kirsty was lying awake, crying silently.

'Kirsty! How are you, Kirsty?' she said quietly.

Her sister turned her back to her and began shaking with sobs. Annie stretched over, but her hand could only rest on her sister's back. She moved off the chair and lay beside her, wrapping her arm tightly around her.

'Kirsty, oh Kirsty.'

'I killed my baby,' Kirsty sobbed. 'I killed my baby.'

'No you didn't. You didn't know what you were doing.'

'I killed him. I threw him away from me. My own baby.'

'No Kirsty, no,' Annie soothed.

'My own baby. I looked at him. I looked on my own baby and I threw him away.'

'Your mind wasn't thinking right.'

Kirsty's body shook and she couldn't speak as sobs heaved through her. Annie pulled closer to her and whispered soothingly in her ear.

'Even when he was growing in me I shut him out.' Kirsty's words were contorted with emotion. 'I told myself I couldn't feel anything and then I tied myself up so tight I didn't let him move. And then when he was born I threw him away. I wish I hadn't. He was just a baby. I killed my bonny baby. I'm his mother, and I killed him.'

'Yes, you were his mother, but you didn't choose to be.'

'But I know now that I loved him as I should have. I looked on my baby, and I loved him. But not enough to stop me doing that.'

'Kirsty, you only did what did because you loved him. You thought you were protecting him from worse things. That shows you loved him.'

'I wish I had jumped with him, then I'd be with him now.'

'Hush, don't talk of such things. We are here for you now and we will help you get strong again. And maybe then you will understand what it was that made you do what you did.'

Kirsty moaned and thrust her head into the bedclothes.

'You're not alone. Me and Mam are here for you. And the doctor will get you well.'

'They've found him, haven't they. They've found my baby. Did you see him? Was he... ?' She couldn't finish the question.

'I didn't see him myself. Dr MacLean said he looked as if he was asleep.'

'I wish I had thrown myself with him. Why did you stop me? I shall be punished.'

'No Kirsty, no.'

'Yes, I will. The policemen were here already. I know. They came with the doctor.'

'I don't think they'll be back.'

'I hope they are. I hope they put me in a jail and let me rot.'

'No Kirsty. The one who should rot is the one who did this to you. You did nothing wrong. He did. He did this to you. He is the one who'll be punished.'

Annie felt Kirsty trembling and held her tighter still. There she waited until Mam came home to help her through the long night ahead.

Grant stared at the document that told him this had been no still birth. It had been murder. The baby had been alive when he hit the waves; not for long, maybe, in the moments it took for the cold to chill his body and the salt water to fill his lungs, but he had been alive.

A pompous, irritating voice broke into his thoughts, instantly nettling him.

'Why would you want a second opinion, Inspector? Pregnancy is not a disease that can confuse. A woman has either given birth or not. Any doctor would know.'

Dr Peter Connolly, too, was an agitated man. He'd had the opportunity for some shooting today and that had been spoiled by the request to travel across the island to confirm what another doctor had already concluded. It was a damned nuisance. He stood before the Inspector, a belligerent, round-bellied man with a trimmed, white beard. Grant had disliked him instantly.

'I want a second opinion, doctor, because I am not satisfied that what I have been told is accurate. It is as simple as that.'

'MacLean is perfectly capable. If he says the woman never had a child, then he is right. There was no need to drag me over.'

'You have made your point, but now that you are here, I would be grateful if you would check the girl. Then you can get back to your more pressing engagements.'

'I don't like your tone, Inspector.'

Dr MacLean interjected.

'I'll take you to the house now.'

'I'm coming with you,' said Grant.

'Very well,' said MacLean.

Grant looked to MacRae.

'You join us, Constable.'

'Rather you than me,' said the town Constable. 'The old fellow has been sour all the way over and the two of them will be at each other's throats.'

On the way to the MacLeods', Dr Connolly had questioned Dr MacLean repeatedly about his examination of Kirsty. He clearly did not doubt his younger colleague. His questions were designed purely to emphasise to Grant the futility of the exercise. The policeman did not even turn his head in response. Out of the corner of his eye MacRae could see him staring ahead, the post mortem report gripped tightly in his hand.

Eventually Connolly fell into a sullen silence, balancing his hands on his stick, which leaned against his stomach. His chin sank so far to his chest that the white whiskers of his beard followed the contour of his belly.

MacRae pulled up the horse at the MacLeod house. He remained on the gig as the other three climbed down, the younger doctor offering support to the stiffer-limbed older one.

As Dr Connolly smoothed down his coat, MacLean spoke to Grant.

'I'd ask that you don't come in with us, Inspector. You'd not be able to watch the examination anyway and I think, with respect, that it would make things easier for all concerned if you stayed here. Dr Connolly will carry out his own examination. If he disagrees with my assessment, then you can come in and cause all the merry hell you want.'

'I'll do what I need to do, doctor,' growled Grant.

Dr Connolly saw a chance to get back at the detective.

'For the moment this is a medical matter,' he asserted. 'I will not have you or anyone in there who might distress the patient.

As Dr MacLean says, if I find any reason to question his findings and I consider the patient is up to it, then and only then can you consider coming in.'

Without waiting for a response, Dr Connolly turned brusquely and walked towards the house then rapped on the door with his stick. Despite the Inspector's visceral dislike of Connolly, he had no reason to doubt that he would be thorough.

The door was pulled open and he saw the mother look at the doctors and then glance beyond them to where he was standing. She was not as surprised by their reappearance as might have been anticipated from someone with nothing to hide.

'Mrs MacLeod,' began Dr MacLean. 'This is Dr Connolly from over in town. I wonder if we might come in?'

The door was pulled wider and the two men removed their hats and stepped in from the light of the day into the gloom of the house. It took the two doctors a few moments for their eyes to adjust. New peats had been put on the fire just a short time before, dulling its glow and making the smoke in the room thicker.

'We'll not keep you,' said Dr MacLean. 'You know why we're here?'

Mam nodded slowly.

'I'll take Dr Connolly through then. Is she in her bed?'

Mam bobbed her head again.

Dr Connolly tried to smile benignly to put the older woman at her ease, but she would only have seen a movement of his whiskers. He saw another girl sitting on a chair in the corner, but she didn't look at him.

'Through here,' Dr MacLean beckoned, then asked Mam, 'Could you pour some hot water into a bowl for the doctor. Thank you.'

Dr Connolly followed him into the bedroom. An oil lamp hardly added to the slight illumination from the skylight. Dr Connolly went over to the bed, removing his coat. A figure lay, apparently asleep and covered up to her neck with blankets. MacLean placed his hand on the shoulder and gently shook it.

'Kirsty. It's me, Dr MacLean.'

Connolly saw there was no jolt or sigh as if the person had

been wakened.

'Remember I told you I might have to come back,' MacLean said softly. 'This is Dr Connolly from town. I would like him to examine you again. It won't take long.'

The girl looked at Connolly.

'Now, now my girl,' Connolly said. 'Just you do as I say and this will be over in no time.'

He whipped back the covers from over her. MacLean stood back. Fear caused the skin around the girl's eyes to twitch.

'Put your legs up girl, will you?' said Connolly rapidly. 'Now then, I'm just going to take a quick look. Nothing for you to be shy about. I've seen hundreds of women.'

MacLean winced. He understood that the older doctor was going through the motions of trying to be kind. But he never once looked at her and even as he asked for her co-operation, he was pulling her into the position he wanted.

'Doctor, could you bring me that water you asked for,' Connolly barked.

MacLean made to leave the room, but Mam was already standing in the doorway holding a bowl of hot water.

'Ah thank you,' Connolly said. 'If you could leave it on that chair and then if I could ask you to leave the room.'

Mam did as she was bade and looked at her daughter.

'Are you alright?' she asked.

Her daughter nodded abruptly.

When Mam had gone, Connolly had pulled back the night-dress and used one of her knees to support his arm as he stared between her legs. He mumbled something to himself and stood up again.

'Damn nonsense this,' he said to MacLean, without looking at him.

He rolled up his sleeves and washed his hands in the bowl of water. Drying his hands on the towel he stepped back to the bed.

'Try to relax,' he said. 'This might be uncomfortable.'

Using the girl's knee as a support again, Connolly leaned forward and thrust his hand between her legs.

She gripped the sheet beneath her. Connolly was twisted in

such a way that his head was looking up to the ceiling, his top teeth biting his bottom lip.

'Relax,' he instructed.

Suddenly he drew back up and crossed the room to plunge his hands into the water.

'That damn fool should have listened to you in the first place,' he said, hardly looking at MacLean. 'This girl has never been with a man, far less had a baby.'

MacLean moved closer to the girl. She had rolled onto her side, crying, and her legs pulled up to her stomach. He pulled the blankets over her and stroked her head.

'That's it. It's over,' he soothed.

Connolly threw the towel down, buttoned up his cuffs and pulled on his coat.

'Come on, doctor,' he said to MacLean. 'That man is going to get his second opinion. And then he's going to get my full opinion.'

'I'll be back,' MacLean said to the girl and quickly followed the older doctor out of the room.

Connolly gave Mam a brisk, 'Thank you, madam' as he walked out of the house. Following behind, MacLean said conspiratorially, 'I'll be back. That should be it over now.'

Sitting by the fire, Kirsty watched the men leave the house.

Epilogue

THE WATER LOLLED AT HER FEET. She had loved that as a child; the initial thrill of the cold and then the gentle massaging, sometimes with a strand of seaweed tickling back and forth. The feet were swollen, hard and contorted now, but the sensation was as ever she remembered it.

She rested now against a black rock that stood alone on the shore as it had done since she had been a wee girl. She remembered it as a test of childhood, when successfully clambering to the top of it marked the coming of a certain age. 'The Beast' they had called it. Sometimes smaller rocks and pebbles clustered around it, at other times it rose clean from a bed of sand. It all depended on the tidal shifts of the Atlantic. In the decades since she had last seen it she had thought that its form might have altered in some way, worn by the batterings of the storms. But no, it was just as it always was. It must have been the same when The Skipper had played on it as a child almost two centuries before, and a thousand years before that the Vikings would have cast their eyes upon it.

She had the eyes of those Vikings, she'd been told. Rheumy with age they were now, but still unmistakably blue. She gazed out to the horizon and back again in time. Eighty-five years she had lived, but her life had blossomed and choked in that one year so long ago. Its shadow had hung over her ever since. The cliffs rising black and broken before her were like some monument to her life, a life that she now sensed was drawing to a close. She was old of course, but more than that she felt her body was slowly closing down. That was what had drawn her to the shore, to see it one last time, while she was still able. She had stayed away for so long because she had feared what she would have to confront within herself.

She had looked upon her son for only a few moments. The pain of her pregnancy had dulled and she had but the vaguest recollections of holding him. She still saw, though, in a muzzy slow motion, the pathetic bundle falling to the sea. But his face she saw in the face of every baby she had looked at in the years that followed. The life that he might have led, she saw lived out by the children who grew around her in the village. Some of them, too, had been taken by a war, and seeing the anguish of loved ones bereft had vividly brought her back to her own grief. Some were alive even yet and she had watched their faces change through the years. Her own child's never had and she remembered and regretted it every day of her life.

There had been no other children because she had never loved again. The man who had been taken from her so long before had been the love of her life, her only love. There could be no other. She had existed for more than sixty years, nothing more than existed, with that love for her Murdo her emotional sustenance. Younger folk might have wondered how this withered old woman could ever have loved. But she had loved, and how breathtaking it had been. It had not evolved over a lifetime into companionship and shared memories. She felt her love for Murdo as vital as it had been on those summer evenings so long before. Even now she talked to him, told him her troubles and reached for him in her loneliness. How remarkable it was, the love of an old, dry woman for a youth, forever fresh and young.

She had never received a telegram. Their bond was not written down for officialdom and she was not his kin. But she had received a letter. When she first saw it, the pencil on lined paper had reminded her so much of Murdo's own that she for a magical moment she thought he was alive and coming back to her. How hard she fell. All hope was crushed by the simple words of a comrade-in-arms.

Dear Miss MacLeod,

It is with deep regret that I write to you. I had a pact with Murdo that if one of us should come off the road the other would write to loved ones. That is why I write. He spoke of you often and of his plans for you both and you were in his thoughts until the last. Murdo was killed on Sunday the 9th. He fell during our advance and died instantly. He would not have known what had happened and he did not suffer. He was a hero and you can be proud of him. Please accept my deepest sympathy in your sore bereavement. I shall write to you again.

Yours sincerely,
Malcolm MacKay

The soldier had never written again. He must have fallen too, although she never knew for sure. It would have meant so much to have been able to speak to him face to face, to know more of how Murdo had been killed and whether he truly knew nothing. She believed that would have made it easier for her to accept his death, but she never did learn of his final moments. Throughout her life she was tormented by the thought of him lying wounded, calling her name and crying for lost dreams. When she learned that the attack on Aubers Ridge had been in vain it was almost too much to bear.

His belongings had been returned to his mother. She asked for Kirsty to come to her one evening in the summer, almost a year after Murdo had first kissed her. Until then, there had been little communication between them, each lost in her own grief. The message was delivered by the brother who had brought her the news those months before. Kirsty gasped when Mam had answered the door to him. 'Can you come to the house?' was all he had said before fleeing, chased away by his own terrible memories.

Kirsty had never been to Murdo's home. Since that morning on the cliffs, she had never even left her own home. It was Mam who forced her to go.

'You can't go hiding away. You must get out.'

Kirsty pulled a shawl tightly around her head and hesitated at the door.

'I'll come with you if you want,' Mam said, 'but I think this is something you should do on your own. It'll be about Murdo.'

That was the impetus to make her step outside, the air so jolting fresh on her face. She couldn't face going through the village, to have people looking at her, talking to her. This would be an ordeal enough. So she walked up the croft and made her way to the house across the moor. Some distance behind her was Annie, ready to crouch behind a peat bank or a rock should Kirsty turn round. Mam had instructed her to follow. Kirsty was watched constantly, even at night. Mam blamed herself for Kirsty's condition and feared what she might do. Annie was relieved when her sister did not take the tracks to the cliffs, but still she followed her closely. She would track her all the way to Murdo's house and back again.

Kirsty came down off the moor onto the road, close to the house. Murdo's house. It was set back from the road and Kirsty hesitated at the stony path. She had passed it before, but then it was just another house in the village. Now she saw the fence posts that Murdo had fixed in place, the thatch that he'd spread and the blue wooden door he had painted. He was everywhere around it. It was only when the door opened and Murdo's mother beckoned to her that she made herself walk towards it.

'Come in, Kirsty, come in,' his mother had said quietly, leading Kirsty into the living room. The fire was out and the house seemed so cold.

'The army,' began Mrs Morrison, 'they sent me Murdo's things.'

A sob suddenly caught in her throat and she fled through to the bedroom. Kirsty remained standing at the table, unsure what to do.

A few moments later she returned holding a parcel in front of her with both hands. Her hands shook as she pulled open the loosely tied knot of string and peeled back the brown wrapping paper. Murdo's few belongings from the Front lay before them. His wristwatch, the glass cracked and the hands stopped. His cap badge with dry mud in the crevices of the mould. Frayed edges of paper poked from his stained, leather wallet. There was the small Bible his mother had prayed would protect him. And there were two small bundles of letters, tied with a bootlace. Kirsty took in every detail.

His mother sat down, her arm resting on the table, supporting her head.

'Some of these letters are yours,' she said wearily. 'Do you want them back?'

Kirsty made an involuntary sound that was neither a word nor a sob, but did not move. Murdo had carried these letters with him when he died. It was their last link. Mrs Morrison picked up one of the packages of letters and handed it across the table to Kirsty. Neither woman could speak. Kirsty wanted to touch his other things, just to feel them in her hands, but this was not her place.

'Would you like a cup of tea?' Mrs Morrison asked eventually.

'No, thank you.' Kirsty didn't want to stay. 'Thank you for the letters.'

'They were yours to have, dear.'

The two fell to silence again and Kirsty just wanted to leave.

'I think I'll go now.'

Murdo's mother nodded absently.

'Thank you,' said Kirsty again and then left.

She didn't feel so close to Murdo in his home. It was not a place they had shared. In the few years that followed before Murdo's mother's passing they never became close. There was a warmth, but it was tempered by Murdo's mother's uncertainty over Kirsty's place in her son's life, and Kirsty's faint, but uncomfortable resentment that his mother stood between her and Murdo.

Annie had watched her leave the house, return to the moor and walk in the direction of the cliffs. Her alarm was quelled when Kirsty sat at the rock that had been the special place for her and Murdo and read over the letters she had sent to him.

Murdo's siblings had grown and carried on with their own lives, but only Alasdair really understood what feelings she had had for his brother. He had tried to be close to her, but emigration had taken him away. Now Murdo's great-grand-nephews and nieces were growing up in the district, maybe seeing him only as a face in a sepia photograph, but never knowing who he was or his love for the quiet old woman who lived further in the road.

She had heard the saying of having outlived one's time and she felt that now, living in a world that even here had changed beyond recognition. But then her time, she mused, had lasted barely nine months. It was a phrase she remembered The Skipper using, and she thought of him fondly. It was he who later told Mam so graphically of the row between the policeman and doctor from town as they had left the house.

'The doctor fellow with the beard came stomping out,' The Skipper had said. 'He went up to the Inspector and asked if he was satisfied. He said MacLean had been right all along and he'd been dragged over from town for nothing. He even told him to go and examine her himself if he wasn't happy. Well, the Inspector said nothing, not a word. He got into that gig and the four of them went back to the police house and not a word was said all the way back. They were saying in the road that the doctor fellow got into yon motor thing and was away over to town straight away.'

Grant had not given up. He had stayed on at the police house with MacRae. Houses were visited and questions asked, but no one had told them anything because no one knew anything to tell. The Inspector had prowled along the cliffs, looking for anything that may have been missed, making minor variations to his route each time.

Mam often saw him near the house. He'd even spoken to her once as she came back from the well. He'd asked how Kirsty was. He said he was sorry that she had been forced through the indignity of being examined twice. He was sorry, but hoped she understood why it had been done. The mother of the baby they'd found, he said, would need help. And he had been so anxious that she got that help that perhaps he had made mistakes. He hoped she was not offended, but he had thought he was doing the right thing by her. If only he could find the girl he could get her the help she must need. Mam had acknowledged what he said and responded in monosyllables. Whatever assurances Dr

MacLean might have given her, the presence of the Inspector was a worry.

It had been a relief when her husband and son returned from the fishing. She was no longer alone. They had heard all about the boys lost and the discovery of the dead baby when they unloaded their catch at the pier. The two men returned to a house suffocated in sorrow. Kirsty's father was helpless to comfort his daughter, but he knew how to protect her. When he learned of the police interest, he made straight for the police house. Kirsty had been scared when she saw him leaving, grim-faced. He never spoke of the confrontation, but the Inspector did not come back.

The investigation just seemed to peter out. Nothing new emerged, no evidence, no testimony, nothing. John MacRae later confided in his wife that the Inspector had believed the case had been solved on that first day. Grant had convinced himself that the answer to the tragedy lay in the house of the three women, but he was never able to prove it. He had discussed his suspicions at length with MacRae.

'They might think it'll all be forgotten,' he'd said over a late whisky the night before he left. 'But they'll be wrong. That was a human being who died. Maybe I can't make them pay for it, but you can't ever forget killing someone like that. That'll live with them and that damned doctor.'

The next day he was gone. Dr MacLean called down at Kirsty's house in a jubilant mood.

'He's gone and he won't be back. It's all over for you now,' he'd crowed.

The investigatin saw the legend of Mary Horseshoe's daughter supplanted. The death of the child had become public knowledge and the culprit a matter of fervid speculation.

'The police thought that Kirsty did it, but they never did know for sure,' Old Peggy had told a gaggle of listeners. 'And do you know why? Because she had nothing to do with the poor child. Two doctors called at that house and that could only be to check that no baby was born there. They checked Kirsty all right from what I hear, but did they check the other one, the quiet one? They did not. For if they had they might have found something.'

'Did you tell the policeman that Peggy?'

'I did not. It's none of my business.'

There were those who came to be convinced that the baby and his killer had indeed come from the house of the twin sister, and that while the police had thought it to be Kirsty, they should have paid more attention to the girl who silently cowered from them.

As she thought back, Kirsty felt the extra burden of guilt that dear Annie had been subjected to, the whispers and the gossip for what was left of her life. She had been taken by the worldwide flu epidemic that had followed the First World War, succumbing to the frothing and the coughing from her lungs. Not for Annie the simple home life that had been her only wish, with a local lad and children of her own in her own village. Instead, this sweet girl's life had ended prematurely in pain and with a stained name. Old Peggy had opined that the Lord could not allow her to escape her awful deed. It was so unfair and cruel.

It had been Dr MacLean's idea that Annie pretend to be Kirsty. He'd come back into the house on that first day when the baby had been found. The policemen were on the cliffs, he'd said, but the Inspector would want to come back with another doctor the next day. Dr MacLean had said that if Annie was willing to impersonate Kirsty, he would see to it that the second doctor would never know. Kirsty had been through enough, he'd said. If they thought she had killed her baby they would not try to understand, they would just send her away. Annie could help her. Her ever-loyal sister had said she would, of course. Dr MacLean had told her that it might not be easy, but he would be there too.

Kirsty had done what she was told by Mam. She had sat by the fire and remembered watching the two men come in and leave again. Mam had immediately gone to see Annie. Her sister never ever spoke of what had happened to her, but Kirsty could still hear her crying, even now. It was one of the many guilts that burdened Kirsty through her days.

In a place where tragedy was part of the landscape, it had been a time of heightened torment. There had been the lads lost at the war, even more after Murdo. Iain Ban had been one of them. The remains of the house that had been his pride still stood. It was a little way down the croft, out of sight of the road. It never was lived in. One gable end remained, standing tall to its apex, the intricate jigsaw of stones withstanding the years of winds and storms. Through the hole that would have been the window, you could see the grass thick and strong. Over the years sheep and cattle had sheltered here and generations of children had played their games, their laughter lifted by the wind. None of them, though, carried the blood of Iain Ban.

A dreadful time. When the war had passed and there was a future again, then, then came the cruel scything of those that remained by the Spanish Flu. And in the village there had been the burning of the doctor's house. Everything but the stone walls had been consumed in an inferno that could not be contained. Futile efforts were made to extinguish the flames as they burst through the windows and beams of the house. No one emerged from the blaze. His charred remains were found in what had been the living room. 'The poor man fell asleep in his chair and a lump of peat rolled off the fire,' was the story that spread round the village. His wife, it transpired, had been away in Glasgow and he had been in the house alone.

Mam was shocked when she heard and brooded over how to break it to Kirsty. Her daughter had been getting better. It had taken years, but when Annie took ill, she nursed her constantly. It was as if Kirsty knew it was her turn to be strong for Annie. What would the news of the doctor do to her? She was outside when Mam came to her.

'There has been a terrible thing happened. I don't know how to tell you, but I have to. Dr MacLean. He's dead. He died in a fire at his house.'

Kirsty remained impassive.

'Oh, what a terrible thing,' Mam sobbed. 'The poor doctor. He was such a kind man. And he was so good to us.'

Kirsty turned and began to move away.

'Where are you going?' Mam asked nervously.

'Don't worry, Mam. I'll be fine. I've work to do.'

Mam watched after her as she walked up the croft.

Kirsty felt frozen inside. She thought back to the morning after the Road Dance when she had lain in the same room as Dr MacLean and saw him asleep by his fireside. She had known him to be a deeply unhappy man and she wondered how much of an accident it might have been. He was a tortured man, a man who struggled to overcome inner demons. Sometimes the drink let them run riot in his head. He had the capacity for tenderness. She knew this to be so; she knew him as her saviour. And she knew him to be her rapist.

In the months that followed the death of her baby he had been so attentive to her and protective of her. He called almost daily, talking to her, leading her from the deep, deep darkness into which she had descended. He made it possible for her to continue her life and tried to convince her that she had been a victim of circumstance. She had chosen to do only one bad thing, he told her, and she had been in no state to make that choice. He was always there for her, to speak to her. He was so kind. But when he had breathed on her the day the police had come, she had known with awful certainty that it was he who had violated her and drawn her to her terrible deed. When he'd spoken to her conspiratorially, she recognised an edge in his voice that she had heard before. The betrayal petrified her. How could he be one and the same man? If he saw the change in her, he gave no indication, but she took care never to be alone with him. He only saw her at the house and her father and brother were near at hand. Over time she feared him less. But the hatred festered.

It had erupted as the flu epidemic began to ebb away. Kirsty was stronger now and the death of Annie was still sore. He had called on one of his visits and they sat on chairs at the end of the house.

'When will it ever end?' he'd asked wearily without expecting an answer.

'It never will,' she'd said. 'We reap what we sow.'

'Kirsty, this has nothing to do with us. What has happened is beyond our influence. And even if it was, you have done nothing. What you did, you did because you were sick. Sickness is not always physical. It can be in the mind too. And like the body, the mind can be healed. You were sick and that is nothing to be guilty about. I thought you understood that now.'

'And what about you?' she asked, her hands clasped tightly on her lap. 'Have you anything to be guilty about?'

'I'm sure I have,' he said half-smiling, but mystified. 'There's none of us perfect.'

'But you're not certain are you?'

'I've done things wrong Kirsty and I've done things I wish I hadn't. I'm no different from anyone else in that.'

'Aren't you? Is every sin the same? Are they all equal?'

'No, of course not. But don't confuse sin and mistakes. I'm just saying that you learn from what you do wrong. You can't torture yourself.'

'What if others are ruined by what you've done?'

'You have to move on, Kirsty. You can't dwell on things.'

'How can you not dwell on things? It's all around us. There are reminders everywhere. Tell me doctor,' Kirsty spat, 'how do you ignore all of that?'

MacLean stared hard at her.

'All these people. My baby. Me. Annie. All destroyed. But we don't dwell on it. We just move on. You just move on.' The bitterness spewed from Kirsty.

Slowly the doctor bowed his head.

'I know it was you. You hurt me. You killed my baby.'

Kirsty had sprung from her seat, but she couldn't bring herself to look at him. MacLean sat for a minute in silence, his shoulders sagging, twisting his hands.

'I am sick, Kirsty,' he said in an undertone. 'The drink. It's an illness for me. There are times when I don't know what I've done. That night. I don't remember. I don't even know why I was there. The drink got the better of me. I am so sorry.'

She stood with her back to him, saying nothing.

'It was when they brought you to me that I realised what I'd done. I don't know what I can say. I've tried to make it up to you. I've tried to put it right, tried to help you recover. Your health, the police, everything. I've tried to make it right.'

'How in God's name could you make it right?' she hissed bitterly. 'What sort of a man would think he could make it better? You've ruined me as a woman. I killed my baby. How could you make that better?'

They both heard the outside door opening. Kirsty stood over the pathetic figure of the doctor.

'You saved me to save yourself and I hate you for it.'

MacLean lurched away from her, unable to bear what she was saying, stumbled past her father in the doorway and out. She never saw him again. The following morning he was dead.

A piece of wood had been floating in the water. Kirsty's failing eyes only noticed when a wave threw it beside her on the shore, leaving it stranded. The wood was part of a packing case that must have fallen from one of the many ships ploughing through the ocean. There were figures burnt on to it, and she stooped to make them out. Above the smaller numbers three initials stood out, N.Y.C. She caught her breath. New York City. On a summer night a lifetime before, she had believed that place would become her home.

She drifted again to that night on the moor as she and Murdo had looked to the glowing sunset in the west and dreamed their dreams. At least she'd had those moments. It was why she had never left. Sometimes, in the late evening, she could see the rise and fall of the knolls on the moor and she could remember with vivid clarity. She felt closer to Murdo, surrounded by the landscape they had known and near to the places that had been special to them. But she could never return to them in person. To do so would be to take her within sight of the cliffs on the other side of the bay and be confronted once again by the unspeakable images they represented.

As the time was slipping away from her, so she found that there was no fear now, only deep regret. A sorrow that she would never know Murdo again. In all those years she had felt his presence with her, looking over her, but she knew that when her time came there would be no celestial reunion.

It was a comfort of the faith that those who were parted

would be together again in the afterlife. Kirsty believed there would be no such peace for her. How could God pardon her when she couldn't forgive herself? She had not even asked in prayer. She had been doomed since that stormy morning when she had cast her child to the waves.

The horizon was obscured now. A grey curtain of rapidly approaching rain sweeping in to envelope all before it. As the first of the raindrops slipped down her cheeks, another wave rolled in, lifted the fragment of wood away from her, and swept it back into the sea.

Some other books published by **LUATH PRESS**

Heartland
John Mackay
ISBN: 978-1-910021-90-3 PBK £7.99

A man tries to build for his future by reconnecting with his past, leaving behind the ruins of the life he has lived. Iain Martin hopes that by returning to his Hebridean roots and embarking on a quest to reconstruct the ancient family home, he might find new purpose. But then he uncovers a secret from the past.

Last of the Line
John MacKay
ISBN: 978-1-910021-91-0 PBK £7.99

When Cal MacCarl gets a phone call to his bachelor flat in Glasgow asking him to come to the bedside of his Aunt Mary, dying miles away on the Isle of Lewis, he embarks on a journey of discovery. With both his parents dead, his Aunt Mary is his only remaining blood link. When she goes he will be the last of the family line and he couldn't care less. In the days between his aunt's death and funeral, he is drawn into the role of genealogy detective.

Girl on the Ferryboat
Angus Peter Campbell
ISBN: 978-1-910021-18-7 PBK £7.99

Forgive
Jenni Daiches
ISBN: 978-1-910021-38-5 PBK £8.99

I loved her from the moment I saw her, and that love has never wavered. It has encased every choice I have ever made, and I have never done anything in my life which didn't involve her image somewhere... I'm so sorry for it all.

A chance encounter on a ferry leads to a lifetime of misplaced opportunities. This is a vividly evoked Scottish tale of chance encounters and of family memories, regret, love and loss. It combines myth, music and linguistics to recount the memory of a hazy summer's day on the Isle of Mull.

Life is a complicated business with no simple fix for damage done. In the face of her ex-husband's need for forgiveness, Ruth wonders about its presence, or absence, in the important relationships of her life, the different things it represents to different people and what it really means to her. On one level, she is uneasy in the role of mother figure, dispensing home comforts to the motley group working out their own life crises under her roof. On another, she deeply enjoys the sense of living family it brings to the old house.

Details of these and other books published by Luath Press can be found at:
www.luath.co.uk

Luath Press Limited

committed to publishing well written books worth reading

LUATH PRESS takes its name from Robert Burns, whose little collie Luath (*Gael.*, swift or nimble) tripped up Jean Armour at a wedding and gave him the chance to speak to the woman who was to be his wife and the abiding love of his life. Burns called one of the 'Twa Dogs' Luath after Cuchullin's hunting dog in Ossian's *Fingal*. Luath Press was established in 1981 in the heart of Burns country, and is now based a few steps up the road from Burns' first lodgings on Edinburgh's Royal Mile. Luath offers you distinctive writing with a hint of unexpected pleasures.

Most bookshops in the UK, the US, Canada, Australia, New Zealand and parts of Europe, either carry our books in stock or can order them for you. To order direct from us, please send a £sterling cheque, postal order, international money order or your credit card details (number, address of cardholder and expiry date) to us at the address below. Please add post and packing as follows: UK – £1.00 per delivery address; overseas surface mail – £2.50 per delivery address; overseas airmail – £3.50 for the first book to each delivery address, plus £1.00 for each additional book by airmail to the same address. If your order is a gift, we will happily enclose your card or message at no extra charge.

Luath Press Limited
543/2 Castlehill
The Royal Mile
Edinburgh EH1 2ND
Scotland
Telephone: +44 (0)131 225 4326 (24 hours)
email: sales@luath. co.uk
Website: www. luath.co.uk